SOMEBODY'S FOOL

SOMEBODY'S FOOL

Adam Kennedy

This first world edition published in Great Britain 1992 by
SEVERN HOUSE PUBLISHERS LTD of
35 Manor Road, Wallington, Surrey SM6 0BW
First published in the U.S.A. 1992 by
SEVERN HOUSE PUBLISHERS INC of
475 Fifth Avenue, New York, NY 10017–6220.

All situations in this publication are fictitious and
any resemblance to living persons is purely coincidental

British Library Cataloguing in Publication Data
Kennedy, Adam
  Somebody's Fool.
  I. Title
  813.54 [F]

  ISBN 0-7278-4369-9

Typeset by Hewer Text Composition Services, Edinburgh
Printed and bound in Great Britain by Dotesios Limited,
Trowbridge, Wiltshire

For Arthur Hadley . . .
with admiration and gratitude

AUTHOR'S NOTE

I have been twice married, once divorced, and I have children. This book, however, is in no way an account of those marriages, that divorce, or those children. *I* am not I; *they* are not they.

The plot moved fast enough
God knows, maybe too fast
for applause or thought . . .

I was forced too often
to ad lib in love, in anger,
Through all, I was given
almost no direction . . .

Worst of all, I was forever
uncertain how to act,
never knowing whether I was
in a comedy or a tragedy.

Anselm Brocki

When I start out to make a fool of
myself, there's very little anyone
can do to stop me. Still . . . everybody's
somebody's fool. The only way to get
over it is to grow old. So I guess
I'll concentrate on that. Maybe I'll
live long enough to forget . . . maybe
I'll die trying.

Orson Welles
The Lady From Shanghai

PART ONE

CHAPTER ONE

I expected to be sooner but it got to be later and later and now of course it's quite late. Better a stale loaf, however, than an empty belly. So for what it's worth, late as it is, here it is now.

Did it surprise you? Since you were there at the abortive beginning, I suppose not. When things started to crumble and get painful and idiotic, I thought often of that festive and drunken, perched-on-cushions dinner near the wharf in your town. You and me and Gwen, and Linda in her blue tube dress with blue beads circling her throat, the scotch in the hotel suite earlier nudging the cathedral chill out of my shins and the wine later simmering it almost completely away until that out-of-nowhere conversation oozed up.

Linda sitting there soft-faced and lovely and singsonging all at once in her little-girl voice that if we should for any reason ever separate she would be entitled to this and that settlement and so much and so on alimony. I laughed, you may remember, made jokes with the Japanese waitress and swallowed down, open-throat, some more saki. But inside me the doubts had started. The war drums had begun to throb.

Back at the hotel after we'd waved you and Gwen away on your two-tone Buick ride to the suburbs, Linda creamed and douched and cologned and black-laced herself into the bed with her baby smile and her legs spread and I turned off the light and said forget it. What is it, sweetheart, she said, all meringue and butter. I can't connect all that alimony and property settlement horse-shit conversation to a wedding night, especially mine, I told her. Don't be silly, she said, I was a little tipsy and that was just talk. Tipsy or not, I said, nothing comes out in words that's not inside already. Don't spoil our wedding night, she said. It's already spoiled, I said, and I didn't do it, you did. Then I went to sleep.

The fact that I slept, that I was able to, may be some reflection on my own hard-nosed, cold-assed nature but I did sleep and so did Linda. We woke up early next day in the soft-gray, ocean-edge morning. Angrily, apologetically, and sweetly at last we consummated our pink-frosting marriage.

I ordered breakfast then on the room phone and when the waiter came he brought a telegram from Dort that said simply and lewdly, "Is it any better now?"

After the waiter left, Linda rolled over against me, gown around her waist, and breathed in my ear the way Lana or Ava must have taught her in some popcorn-littered matinée theater in Newark one sixth-grade day. It *is* better, she said and I said yes, you're right, it is. But it wasn't. It was good. Great even. But no better than it had been in her apartment on Sixty-fourth Street or in my apartment on Eighty-second Street or in that portable turmoil of a whore-house-with-swimming-pool-hotel on Argyle in Hollywood. Or in the motel outside San Diego that weekend we went to Tijuana with John and Evelyn and had a crazy lock-up on a wide bed with an orange bedspread and a mirror on the wall at the foot.

As nearly as we could figure later, Linda got pregnant that afternoon on the orange bed. Second time. She had got pregnant before on the puppy-stained, wall-to-wall carpet in her New York apartment on Sixty-fourth Street ten days after I went there for the first time and we drank scotch on the rocks till she said it was coming out of her ears.

She drank well then. Not at all like later in our house by the ocean (that's where we called from when your twins were born) when she got on the sherry prescription (her own) and closed every day in pink-eyed shrillness, wedging herself in the bedroom door and blocking my exit from that last refuge to the last-plus-one, the empty beach.

Cute and sticky, another uncomfortable half-baked scene out of a summer double feature, the way she announced her pregnancy to me that first time. I had known her then for six weeks. She handed me a small, delicately-wrapped box. Then she mixed me a bomber drink and we sat down. She said open it. She kissed me and smiled and big-eyed me and I opened it. Inside were two satin, embroidered and frightening baby shoes and a white card with a ribbon laced through it, the same kind we sent later when each of our boys was born, and on the card she had written, "To daddy from mommy." The situation called for soft words and more of the free-wheeling, uncontracepted same.

Lying beside me later in her pale blue negligee, not *in* it, really, but over her, over us (she always wore it when I came to see her, every time after the first time), with me stroking her silky, flowing, tinted-since-the-age-of-eleven hair, and thinking of Urda and my sixteen-month-old daughter in Nassjö.

So I lied to Linda. Again. I had told her from the beginning about Urda, that we were married, that there was Ingergerd, a daughter. A camouflage lie to be wheeled out when needed as it was now and bolstered by the additional lie that a Swedish divorce would take at least a year even if I asked Urda immediately. "Won't you ask her?" Linda said. "Of course I will," I said. Lying again on top of a lie but feeling guiltless then as I do now because I *felt* married to Urda. I had always since that crazy black-damp day outside Göteborg with me tossing pebbles at her legs as we all waited for the bus and Wade who sensed I was after her before I knew it myself saying, "You must be in love, Jim. That's the way eight-year-olds show their affection." By saying that and by trying to make me look, that afternoon, like a jackass, he crystallized something that both Urda and I had tried to ignore, because of Stig and because of three-year-old Arvid. Hearing Wade label it took away the hestitation.

That night I waited for her in the tree-shadows beside the dining hall. She slipped out of the hotel in her night-gown and found me there in the dark. And Wade, the loud-mouthed, sarcastic son-of-a-bitch, spent the rest of the summer, until he'd finished his role in the picture and headed back to Paris, thinking I was a world's champion prick because I was breaking up a happy home.

What Wade didn't know and what nobody knew except me was that I wasn't stealing Urda from her husband. I was stealing her from a cigar-smoking shipbuilder from Stockholm who had stolen her long ago from Stig. I never met him but I smelled his cigar smoke in her hair many times that summer in Sweden after she'd promised to give him up.

I wrote to Urda last month after Linda landed in New York from Juarez fondling her Mexican decree and searching the airport crowds for the bland face of new-husband-to-be.

When Urda wrote back, her letter was warm and good and full of news of eight-year-old Ingergerd. It was almost

6

as though my six-and-a-half-year silence hadn't happened. A couple of letters later she said she thought we should write of course because of our daughter and because of a lot of things that had happened to us together but she wanted me to understand that though she hadn't seen him for a long time, the cigar man was still what she wanted, what she had always wanted. "This thing in me will not change. I know it now."

I also know it now and I wish I'd known it then but I didn't. And I didn't know it when I was lying on the sofa with Linda, the baby shoes on the low table beside us and a lot of words being said about how we'd work it out. She would go to Europe, we decided. I would make some money somehow, then follow her. And after the quote divorce unquote from Urda, Linda and I would get married. In Italy, for example. Because she was so happy to have a fetus inside her for the first time (I assume it was the first time because she said so but she also told me about a series of ferocious hemorrhages six months before which she called heavy menstruation but which sounded to me, old hand at the game, like post-abortion or post-miscarriage hemorrhage), she would have smiled and accepted any plan, farfetched, impractical, and international runaway though it might be.

"Italy," she said, "we'll have a lovely baby in Italy. And I'll be Mrs. James Tyler."

Three days later she fainted under the blistering lights of a hurry-up photographer on East Fifty-third Street and coming to, was persuaded to pose in just one more peignoir before, trembling and white-eyed, she flagged a Third Avenue cab and struggled home. When I arrived at the apartment late in the afternoon, the baby-to-be-born-in-Italy had long since been flushed away and Linda lay pale and spent on her back-breaking convertible sofa-bed.

CHAPTER TWO

The baby shoes put away somewhere or other in her sweet-scented, pack-rat storage system, we took up our cocktails at five, dinner at nine, bed at eleven, love affair from then (it was January) until June when I went to Boston to do a summer play and ended up a week later, first in Annapolis, then in California, doing a picture for Dort's husband, the perverted, ego-ridden director. Greek. Dort called him that, nothing else, The Greek.

"I saw the thing you did on television last month – the paralyzed convict. Excellent."

The stark truth of the matter (although I *was* quite good as the paralyzed convict), the true reason for hiring me and bringing me to California, it titillated the sick bastard to see me with his wife. He knew about us from the Chicago days when Dort had divorced the sugar broker and farmed her daughter out to an aunt in St. Louis, leaving herself free to gin rummy and vodka and lie under me in my furnished room on the near north side. He knew because she had told him. And she *may* have told him, if not he guessed, that when she telephoned him every afternoon when he was in Milan and she was apartmented in the Lancaster in Paris, I was athwart her as they exchanged international pleasantries.

The baby shoes away and me going ahead to greater and grander things (another Gary Cooper, my agent said tentatively. The casting director replied that every agent in town has another Gary Cooper. He's really more of a Jimmy Stewart type said my agent, creative and tenacious. Uh-huh, said the casting man, overweight, ugly, and clearly losing interest), my Sixty-fourth Street (or Eighty-second Street if we chose my apartment for variety) arrangement with Linda might well have died a graceful death. Not, however, for lack of interest on my part. In spite of my cruel tongue, sharpened by the perspective of a cool marriage and a hot divorce, I admit to you and myself and to all the curious that I was idiotically involved with Linda. The pelvis has reasons that reason knows nothing of. This might well serve as my epitaph. Or yours. If my memories of college are accurate, you and that pale and silent heiress from LaGrange were envied for your midnight access to the dissection tables in the zoology laboratory.

L'Université. Long gone. I saw Howie Brightman eight years ago, here in New York. Did I tell you this at wedding time? He was bloated and cynical, divorced long since from Bonny (I later heard from her, she wrote me in California after seeing me on a television show, and said they were divorced because Howie, with a full-blown mania about getting her pregnant, scared to death of it, had finally stopped sleeping with her altogether), and drinking double shots of bourbon. Making a lot of money, flying his own Cessna around the south and selling something-or-other for some sheet-metal company. Later on he wrote and told me he'd married a widow lady with four children and had had himself tied off so he could shoot nothing but blanks. How do you figure that one?

When I saw him here in New York, all puffy and screwed-up and drinking like an idiot, I felt responsible for him in a way. We roomed together that last year in

9

school (you were gone) and he thought I was a big man and tried to be like me. Or so his mother told his sister who told her roommate at the Alpha Chi house who told J.J., who told me. But for Christ's sake that was a long time ago, and responsible or not I can't shed tears now for those dead days, can I? I think not. Stitching yesterday and today and tomorrow together, that's my survival activity now.

Also while I'm feeling sorry for Howie I know very surely that if he could see me here in New York, flubbing the dub, going nowhere except to Fordham Road three times a week to see my kids, trying to scrub away the residue of seven years wasted in a marriage that wouldn't get off the loveless ground, years squandered in a dollar-conscious desertion of everything I am and want to be, he would feel genuinely and gigantically sorry for *me*.

Do you get the Alumni magazine (or have you succeeded in covering your tracks?) with the swollen, jowly, hard-eyed portraits of our contemporaries (not our peers), all of whom are becoming or have become already executive advisory sales-manager assistants to the presidents of toilet-bowl factories? With unlimited expectations, profit-sharing, health and wealth plans, names stencilled on parking spaces, and solid-gold, monogrammed, engraved cuff links that really flush. Oh, gloom. Tell me, old friend, would you prefer to fall down, snap your spine, and be carted off to the incinerator while attempting a dance step (beautiful, intricate, and impossible) of your own devising or would you rather reach the pinnacle in Hamilton, Ohio, for your ability to execute faultlessly and on cue, the first four well-diagrammed steps of a fox trot? If there's more than one answer to that question, I'll kiss all the asses from here (East Fifty-eighth Street,

10

New York City) to Altoona, Pennyslvania (Is that in the bituminous belt?) and back.

What the hell all this has to do with you, or me, or Linda or anything at all now that life is serious and adult and frayed around the edges I'm not sure. But if the grace notes are unnecessary and if the grafitti on the bricks can be painted over or chipped off and not be missed then I don't want to play the kazoo anymore and I'll give up, from this day forward, writing on walls. Do you know what I mean? Probably not.

CHAPTER THREE

Do you think the fact that Gwen was held up in traffic on the inbound and didn't get to the cathedral until the ceremony was half over and we had to enlist the vicar's Australian wife to serve as matron of honor contre your epic best man may have been perhaps an omen that things would end, for Linda and me, less wonderfully than planned? I jest, of course. I dig not omens. Or talismans. Or amulets. Or weddings, for that matter. Not no more.

The vicar's wife, or perhaps she was the sexton's wife, dowdy but upright and well-intentioned, insisted that it was the best of all possible signs. Stranger at the wedding, she crooned, very fine. Since she lived there on the grounds, I have come to believe that the stranger was in reality not she but me. The Reverend, I suspect, would support me in this. In spite of his open-faced murmurings of the dogma, his warm stories of touch football with the young parishioners, and ingenuous tales of his own camp-out honeymoon in the Sierras, I suspect strongly that he put politics ahead of faith, collection ahead of instruction, and himself ahead of me, all grievous sins. I firmly believe also that he, fraud or not, firmly felt that I was a fraud. Linda liked him. She liked him very much. Thought he was cute.

Linda *didn't* like you much. Should I not tell you this?

Why not? I am sure that neither your self-confidence nor your ego will suffer. How did she find you? Clever? Yes. Intelligent? Yes. Amusing? Certainly. Hates all those things. I never know what he's thinking, she said. Why in the world should you, I said, unless he tells you. Well, you know what I mean. He's sarcastic. He happens to have a marvelous wit – I defended you – severe sometimes but never malicious. "You know what I really can't stand about him?" she said at last. Brace yourself. This may tear away all the pilings you've built on these thirty-odd years. "I can't stand men who wear brown shoes."

Albert Einstein, Pablo Casals, Matisse, Heifetz and a few others I called forth, asking if they would suffer in her estimation if caught somehow, somewhere, in an unguarded moment, in shoes of brown. That's different, she said, and with that blistering coup of logic ended the discussion.

'That's different' and 'you know what I mean' are the two ultimate arrows in the female quiver. Do you agree? Can you possibly sit there in your citadel of brown-shod sarcasm and say me nay? No matter. Let's press on to a brighter plateau.

Jackie Dehner. How's that for openers? In nineteen something or other I met a girl in the New York Central bar car between Indianapolis and Chicago who knew Jackie, said she had married some dull fellow in securities, as I remember it, and was working as a gray lady at Passavant Hospital two afternoons a week.

Jackie once said something to me that stuck in my head. We were walking from my dingy cave on Huron Street where we had undoubtedly been bedded although my specific memories of naked activity with her are set in that apartment of her sister's on North State Parkway. It was winter and colder than hell, I remember the gray fur coat she used to wear, and we stopped there where the brownstones end at the edge of that cinder parking lot, where you and I used to pass a football around on Saturdays. She was whining at me about one thing or another, she probably liked me the least of any girl I ever knew, and finally she said – this is the part I remember – "You're not conceited exactly. You're just self-aware."

The aptness of this judgment (if she'd been honest or perhaps more articulate, she'd have told me I was a double-dealing son of a bitch because that's what, it came out eventually, she really thought of me) I will leave to the angels. But I *was* struck at the time by her turn of phrase.

To show you there's hay to be made from a chance encounter on the New York Central, the girl I met who told me about Jackie also mentioned that her father wanted to sell his Cadillac (like new, etcetera). So I told Kermit Givener (did you ever meet him) who was a merchandising director at our offices, he called the girl at her home in Oak Park, trained out there the next weekend and bought the car. It was a bargain, the girl's father was moving to Barbados, so Kermit, in gratitude, took me to the Walton Hotel Men's Grill and bought me a two-hour lunch with five martinis, cognac, et al. And three weeks later, the Cadillac exploded and killed him. I'm joking. It was really a very good car. I rode in it that spring all the way out to Comiskey Park. I had to take the lousy elevated home, however, since Kermit lived on the south side and didn't want to drive me back north after the ball game.

Back to Jackie. In my opinion, she was bloody boring as a playmate or a mistress or what-have-you. I realize you may not agree since, deny it though you will, you were standing at the ready to jump on her when she and I gave up our pitiful little affair, that night when the three of us were drinking gin in her sister's apartment and she and I had a quarrel and I left alone.

Ah-ha! Just to show you how faultless my memory is, I remember now as I'm sticking this together that the true situation was very nearly the reverse of that. The first time *I* made it with her, the three of us were platonically drinking in the apartment when I, scenting game, secretly urged you to go and you, loyal friend, went. So did you screw her or didn't you?

For all her faults, I liked Jackie in a way. I always enjoyed talking with her as long as she didn't answer. I felt sorry for her, too.

Was it Rimbaud who said, "I have a great advantage over other men. I have no heart." Or was it Rilke or Racine or Verlaine? Or was it you? Not me. Although I admit I have been so accused. Who, having gone to the lists with the succulent female has not. On my headstone, I will ask that there be chiseled the following legend – "He did what he could."

CHAPTER FOUR

The first time I met Jackie was the same weekend I met you (I assume I met you because I stayed there at the fraternity house as a guest. There's no gleaming incident, however, in my memory that features you. Sorry.) and the first weekend, in fact, that I visited the university.

Does the chronology begin to come clear now in your intricate mind, honeycombed as it is with classical references, irregular verbs, and quiescent lecheries? You were at the close of your first college year, I was finishing my term at an obscure art school in Chicago. I think that time of fatigue, frustration, and loneliness set to my life a permanent pattern of furnished rooms, bathrooms down the hall, stale cornflakes, boloney sandwiches, and french fries out of a brown paper bag onto an oil-cloth tabletop. It became my way.

Since I made my whore's decision (I was walking with Jess down the Rue de la Gaité and I said – somebody's going to be making those cowboy movies so it might as well be me) I have in good years paid as much money to an accountant to make out my tax forms as I would have needed in the oilcloth days for complete living expenses for six months. My oldest son, Gregg, first faced life, to quote a feeble-minded fan magazine, "in a hillside mansion in Encino." His younger brother, Arthur, came home from the hospital to plate-glass modern, overlooking the Pacific, and their mother, fragile Linda, lived, if not luxuriously, in a way that may have distorted forever her barely-formed sense of the reasonable.

And all the while, the booted, sombreroed idiot, me, who had never had a private bathroom till age thirty-two (the apartment on Eighty-second Street), was longing back to the furnished rooms, the black hole on Huron Street with the blue plush chair, dust like a thick-piled carpet, the gin-guzzling maid, and a fake fireplace abloom with rubber ferns, gift from a lady decorator with prematurely grey hair who came to spend an hour and stayed six weeks, leaving at last only when the dust, my studied infidelity, and the highly vocal ménage à trois next door threatened to unhorse her completely. The next stop, an ocean away, the seventh floor trudge-up in Montparnasse where in four years most of the tides I will know in my life began to run in me, where my wheel, if hubbed anywhere, is hubbed. Where Ingergerd was conceived, where Deirdre broke her what-about-my-mother chains by simply taking off her red angora sweater that had shed on my chest like blood streaks, dropping her skirt to the tiles and sliding white and slow into the hollow at the center of the bed. Where her aunt Caroline then broke with her niece and with her own sister, Deirdre's mother, by being whiter and less slow. Until she left for Florence on the second leg of her six-week, man-eating tour of Europe. Deirdre came back then but not for long. I had killed her mother for her and Caroline had killed me and it wasn't any good for her anymore. So she took her red angora sweater and her pale swan's body (she called me the dragon) and boarded the *wagon-lit* for Rome. I heard later that she was engaged to an Italian acrobat, that she was very happy, and that she worked all the time dubbing Italian films into English. I saw her in Chicago three years later, she must have been about twenty-six by then, and the candle had gone out behind her eyes. She was an old lady when I met her but she started to get young for a minute or so. Now she was an old lady again.

She had made a big thing of it there in Paris once I'd got her started. She wanted to be tied to the bed and blind-folded and abused and all the four-letter words. But she never really enjoyed it. That kind never does. Or maybe I was no good for her. *Quien sabe?* And who, at this point, gives a damn? I tried to call her last time I was in Chicago. After the divorce, of course. No adulterer I. I found her name in the book and dialed her number and a young guy answered. I said is Deirdre there and he said (hot young love) who's calling her? So I told him, calling myself Mr Tyler so he'd think I'm a harmless old cocker, and he said (a bit relieved but still spooked-up), she works for Delta Airlines, you can call her there. I tried her there, couldn't reach her, left my name and said I was at the Osmond Hotel (big spender). In two minutes an unfamiliar voice called, anxious, breathy, mystified, and said, "This is Deirdre so-and-so." I said, sorry, you're the wrong Deirdre so-and-so and hung up.

CHAPTER FIVE

Deirdre's aunt Caroline, also in Chicago, still looks able but feels otherwise, I suspect. She always wore long-legged panty girdles, which is an indication of something or other and her approach to the act though willing, even aggressive (especially in Paris or when scotched-up) was profoundly straightforward and academic. She was disinclined to experiment, dawdle, or go ape.

She had a dog. Sweet enough. Friendly and reasonable. Well trained not to bark, bite, or slobber, but nonetheless, a disturbing element to me, especially when I was in bed in classic position with big Caroline.

Dogs. You remember Dad Westerfield, don't you, the hook-shot artist from the Phi Delt house? Perhaps you didn't know him too well at school. I didn't. But he and I were at Randolph Field at the same time (if my agent had this information, she could figure out my real age. A hundred and eight. Not that she gives a damn) and I got to know him there. Then after I was discharged and back at the university, I used to see him whenever he was home on furlough. He broke up with that Kappa, Bugsy whatever-her-name-was, and she and I had a big extra-curricular, late-date thing going for a while. Dad was a little hot about that until he found out that the real villain was a chap from Bugsy's hometown, a draft-dodger at Northwestern. Then we, Dad and I, were friends again.

We were at the Panther Room in Chicago a year or so later. I had a date, a bimbo from my hometown, and Dad didn't. So he danced with my girl a few times. He told me afterwards that she'd asked him to meet her later that night after I took her back to her hotel. He said, "But naturally I wouldn't do that to a buddy," and I said, "Uh-huh." If he still had a burr about me and Bugsy, that little incident in the Panther Room apparently healed all his wounds. Assuming it actually happened and it probably did. Because the girl (my date) was a genuine pig. Attractive in a kinky sort of way, but a pig. I ran into her in my hometown when I came back from Europe. I hadn't seen her in six or seven years. I took her to some out-of-the-way fifth-rate hillbilly music emporium and rib joint and bought her a Seagram's and Seven or two (big drink in Missouri, also Mogen David and Seven-Up. And they drink scotch with coke. Scout's honor.) then strolled her along afterward to the public gardens near the ball park where she unbuttoned her mink-dyed muskrat coat, it was April and cold as hell, lifted her skirt like a lady and pumped me on the wet grass under the lilac bushes. She was much better there, cold ground and all, than she had been in bed in the Allerton Hotel in Chicago.

Anyway, Dad and I used to see each other pretty often after the war and after we graduated when I was working for the friendly furniture folks and he was travelling around the Midwest for General Foods and getting into Chicago every month or so. You were still there part of this time, I guess, but most of the time I was seeing Dad, you had already rolled off to California.

He and I took a vacation together one summer and spent a couple of weeks in Nassau and the next year we were planning to go someplace together again. But we screwed up our schedules somehow. My vacation started a week before his and his ended a week after mine. Also Dad had to get down to Okeefenokee country to see some dolly he had staked out there by the swamp. Maybe that's why he made his vacation later – I don't remember.

Anyway, we decided that I would kill time for a few days, I guess I went home to see my folks, then I would meet Dad and we'd swoop off somewhere for a week after which he would go on to Okeefenokee and I would go back to Chicago to sweat. What I'm getting to is the dog story.

We drove down through Kentucky and Tennessee and ended up one night in Gatlinburg. Next morning (it was July Fourth and all the rednecks were down from the hills in their heavy blue suits and print shirts) we drove up into the Smoky Mountains and found an out-of-the-way, clapboard, front-for-a-still hotel and we moved in for a week of booze, branch water, and fresh air. Under sixty years of age there was nobody there but us. The following morning, however, there appeared in the dining room (unlikely, disturbing vision) two pale file clerks on a fling from Akron, Ohio.

These girls had eyes, noses, lips, ears, breasts, bottoms, legs and all the rest of it. But the quantities, the proportions, the relationship of each element to its neighbour was too original in concept to qualify. "When they start to look good to us," Dad said, "it will be time to move on."

Dissolve to the following afternoon. Dad missing. After waiting two hours I walked through the woods a way and, hearing laughter, Indian-footed through the bushes to a spot beside the creek where Dad and the two Akron gems were disclosed, giggling, feet awash, steadily pouring beer into their warm bellies and tossing pebbles at the floating empties.

"I admit yours is a dog," Dad said at dinner time, "but

mine is not too bad, so the least you can do is keep the other one out of my hair."

"That's the least I can do?"

"Seems that way to me," Dad said.

"What's the most I can do?"

"Have a little fun, Jimbo. She's not that bad, is she?"

"Yes."

So after dinner I ended up in the back seat of Dad's convertible with Betty Akron beside me singing folk songs (actually she sang pretty well) and Barbara Akron up front with Dad. He was making tired jokes and trying to get her to laugh but she just sat there, silent and smoking. I thought at least mine has some personality (thus self-deception begins), but *his* is a fish. So I sang the harmony on a couple of folk songs and Betty said I was pretty good and so forth and so on and Dad even squeaked out a few sad notes. Since he's tone deaf his singing didn't help matters much. His girl kept fogging those cigarettes until the smoke, even with the car windows open, was beginning to dry out the membranes in my nose. Dad started clearing his throat then and drumming his fingers on the back of the front seat. I knew he was suggesting that I take the folk singer for a stroll across the pine needles while he worked the front seat to see if there was any fire behind all that smoke. So I did.

Cut to a moonlit glade, two hundred yards from the car (the tone-deaf bastard couldn't say I didn't give him enough elbow room) with me and the folk singer sitting on a stump singing and chattering and killing time. I thought, it's too bad she's such a beast because this is, I must admit, a hell of a spot with the soft grass and the crickets going at it and the moonlight and all. And she is kind of a sweet kid. So I thought what the hell and I kissed her. Right away, I knew I'd made an error. As soon as I touched her she

22

started to tremble and hang on to me like she was going under water and I knew she was surely as innocent as hell. On the other hand, she seemed determined to be less innocent if someone would cooperate. Enter the dog.

As soon as we sat down on the stump, this dog had come plunging out of the dark, shaking all over and wagging his tail and rubbing up against our legs and trying to get himself scratched or petted or whatever it was he wanted. There was enough light so I could make him out. He looked like an Airedale, not quite full grown. I gave him a cuff on the side of the head and said, "Lay down," not because I can't conjugate the verb "to lie" but because I think it's best to speak to a dog in the language he's accustomed to.

"Oooh," she said, "you hurt him." "No, I didn't," I said, "I just want to be sure he doesn't hurt you." As you know, my friend, once you start the horse-manure with women, you can't always turn it off, even when you'd like to.

"Ooooh," she said again and squeezed my arm with fingers made strong from opening and closing file cabinets. We talked and harmonized a little more with no interruptions from Airedale and that was when I kissed her.

Being a roué, a man of parts, as you are, or were in those days, I'm sure you appreciate better than I could explain, the chemical and emotional cross currents that buffeted me, in a few moments, from a cool position of sitting-on-a-stump-don't-careism to a not-so-cool kneeling position beside a pale Akron candidate, naked, partially by my hand, mostly by her trembling own, and half-reclining against the rough hide of our stump seat.

An idyll? Le Déjeuner sur L'herbe? Read on.

Have I painted the scene completely? A soft night, the scent of fir and pine and balsam, a shadowy moon, a

23

sheltered grass carpet under the trees, and two chaste, silvery forms coming together in the dimness.

One half-breath short of the beginning, I sensed a whir of movement behind me and a furry, wet-tongued weight landed on my back. The Airedale. Friend, companion, servant? All right. *Voyeur?* Why not? *Numéro trois in a ménage à trois?* I think not. Not if I'm *numéro deux.*

So it ended. Not blissfully. Not dramatically or tenderly. Idiotically.

Can you picture me, summer visitor to a southern state, tired commercial brain in search of rest, hopping about in the moonlight, naked as a python, swearing and kicking at a disillusioned dog? Does it amuse you? It amused the girl, almost to apoplexy. And it amused me, too, finally. We sat on the grass naked and laughing, our stomachs hurting from it, our arms round each other like children. After a while we got dressed and walked hand in hand back to the hotel, still laughing in explosive bursts.

We spent the next four days together and we had a nutty time. I really liked her. We laughed like a pair of fools right up to the moment when Dad and I drove her and her friend down to Gatlinburg to catch the bus. We really laughed. And that's all we did. Dad didn't even do that. That odd girl just kept smoking and looking at him as though *he* was the ugly one (Dad, as you may remember, is one handsome son-of-a-bitch) and *she* was the catch. Personally, I think he used bad tactics, but that's history now. The girl was probably sleeping with her boss back in Akron.

CHAPTER SIX

Because I know you're a romantic fellow and because I'm sure you've developed compassion, just as I did, for my laughing folk singer who was done out of her summer triumph by a horny Airedale (next morning she whispered to me, "I'll never like Airedales again." Good girl. Ugly as hell and inclined to sweat, but a fine, good girl) I must finish her story. Truth, nothing but truth, and stranger, far stranger, than made-up stories.

After what I've told you, what would you say the odds would be that I might see her again? I didn't know her last name (I *had* known it, of course, but it had slipped away) and I don't know it now. I had no idea of her address other than somewhere in Akron. She knew my name but nothing else about me, only that I lived in Chicago. We had no mutual friends other than Dad who knew no more about her than I did. The odds? Ten thousand to one. At least.

All right, suppose somehow we did run into each other? That could happen. But if it did, what about the odds that we might catch up the summer reins and miraculously finish what had been interrupted in a moon-washed Tennessee clearing months before? The odds must be a million to one against that.

Now you sense the ending; I'll go swiftly with the details. Dad in Chicago for a convention between Christmas and

New Year's. Staying at the Palmer House. Come down, he says, I've got a bottle, we'll drink a while. Five-thirty, I arrive. I saw her, he said when I walked in, your ding-dong friend from the Smoky Mountains. Are you sure? What would she be doing here? I don't know, but I'm sure I saw her in the lobby. What was her name, do you remember? No, do you?

So we forgot about her and drank for a while and shot the breeze and told lies about how well we were doing in our jobs. Then suddenly Dad pointed his finger at me and said "Stone" and I said "What?" and he said, that's her name, I'm sure that's her name. I said maybe . . . I don't remember. So he picked up the phone and said "Miss Stone's room, please." Then his face got red and he waggled the receiver at me and said, "I told you so. They're ringing her room."

He said, "Miss Stone? Excuse me, Miss Stone, but weren't you in Gatlinburg, Tennessee last summer? (pause) I thought so. Well, this is Dad Westerfield, bla-bla, and why don't you come up here for a drink? About ten minutes? Fine."

He hung up and we started spluttering and cuffing each other and hopping around like a couple of storks until all of a sudden the buzzer buzzed and Dad whispered, "Hide in the bathroom. She doesn't know you're here."

I ducked into the bathroom and closed the door and Dad let her into the room. I heard them laughing and talking, ha-ha and all the rest of it. Small talk is not Dad's long suit. I knew he'd run out of gas in that area pretty quick.

In a few minutes, just as I'd expected, he came into the bathroom to get water for a couple of drinks, kicked the door shut behind him, and whispered, "You wait a few more minutes, Jimbo. I'll start her talking about you, then you come out, and she'll fall over." (Corny? You bet.)

"How's she look?" I said. "Better than last summer," Dad said. "How does she *look*, Dad?" "Terrible." he said.

So I marched out of the bathroom after a while. I didn't even feel like a jackass which will give you some idea of what a jackass I was. She didn't fall over but she certainly turned red. Dad quickly put her at her ease by loading her drink and after a while her face got back its normal paleness.

She didn't have a chance. Or maybe I didn't have a chance. However you want to look at it. Someone, at our births, had put an X on each of our stomachs and said, "They've got to get together." So we did. Later that night in her room. And to show you how smart and wise and perceptive I am, she wasn't a virgin after all. Not technically. But she really trembled and she was really inept and she really meant what she was doing. I felt like the world's champion bastard. Uncontested. She didn't know the rules or the name of the game even but she was in there flying on instruments and trying to be a good kid. I felt smooth and experienced and reptilian. And old. I've felt old since I was eighteen.

Linda was always at me to buy a dog. "A puppeeee," she called it. Not with transient families or in apartments. If you take them on (all this I said to Linda) they're your responsibility just as a child is. And always she answered me, "But I *want* a puppeeee!" Now that she doesn't have me, perhaps she'll get one.

CHAPTER SEVEN

Furnished rooms. The man, more specifically, my vagrant friend, Millard Hofer, said, speaking of the novel, "There comes a moment, all the critics having been heard, all the theories having been expounded, all reputations having been shattered, reference reading finished and notes taken, awards given and received, tea or cocktails sipped, children diapered, hugged, and admonished, wives kissed and fondled, when the novelist must enter a bare room in an expensive hotel, close the door behind him, hang up his coat, take a leak, stare out the window, rumple his hair, and at last sit down in sharp-pencilled silence and do his work."

More from Hofer:

Neighbor: Where's your brother this morning?

Girl: He's in the room there.

Neighbor: But the door's closed. (trying it) It's locked.

Girl: Yes.

Neighbor: What is he up to in there?

Girl: He's working.

Neighbor: All by himself?

Girl: Yes.

Neighbor: (after a pause) Does he *like* to be alone like that?

Girl: He has to do his work. He's a poet, you see.

Neighbor: (listening) I don't hear a sound. Are you *sure* he's working?

Girl: He said he was going to work.

Neighbor: And does he go in that room every day?

Girl: Most days, yes.

Neighbor: Strange. Very strange.

Girl: But why are you crying?

Neighbor: I feel so sorry for the poor thing.

Girl: My brother?

Neighbor: No. Your mother. How sad it is to have a weird child.

Before I got the apartment in New York on East Eighty-second Street, my first private bath, age thirty-two (see above) I lived in a furnished room on West Ninety-third. Actually unfurnished until Dort fitted it out with sleek odds and ends from her inexhaustible storage lots. (She was still my patron saint then, doting sponsor, and occasional bed-mate when nothing else was going for her. I must point out that there is no censure in that observation. I loved Dort uncontrollably for three months, was fond of her for ten years, and always enjoyed making love to her. Flat-chested as a child, she was nonetheless very much a woman, with a bizarre tilt to her pelvis which is, in my experience, unique, and though the language we once spoke together is now a dead one, I think of her, when I think of her at all, as a childhood friend who moved to another city.) I then covered the slate-grey walls with ripolin-on-plywood paintings from my one-man exposition in Paris in the gleaming early winter of another year.

I didn't accomplish all that much work on Ninety-third Street. I did some drawings and attended an acting class twice a week; I went to South America on a job that spring and when I came back I sat on the roof outside my window in the hot New York August and got freckles and a suntan and talked on a long-corded telephone. I was starting

29

on a meandering, rootless, penis-directed, money-twisted
ramble into the fog that I haven't reached the end of yet.
I met Linda that fall and, point of reference in your life,
I saw Dolly Corso again in the spring of that year.

Did you know I *went* (isn't that a great word for it) with
Dolly? It was when I was fresh back from the air corps and
you were still in the navy. Now that I've carefully located
you in time and space, you must wait and Dolly must wait
because some nagging tic in the grey folds of my brain tells
me that I did not finish with Jackie Dehner.

CHAPTER EIGHT

It mystifies me that I should dwell on Jackie at such length. Objectively, she was a tight-cunted Pekinese with delusions of her own importance, a type who writes anonymous letters, slashes paintings, and buries knives in the stomachs of sleeping males. But such is the measure of my concern and compassion for my fellow human creatures.

That first spring weekend I spent at the university, I drove down from Chicago with our rich fraternity brother, George Armand. Does it begin to come back to you now?

George was in graduate school at the University of Chicago, refresher to your memory, and I was waiting tables there at night to support my art classes in the daytime. I talked to him a few times as the months went past and in the spring he said, "Why don't you drive down to my old university with me next weekend?" I said "why," and he said "I think you should give up this art school crap and get yourself a college degree." I said, "no money," and he said "there are scholarships to be had." And then he said "it's an excellent school – lots of gorgeous girls."

So I drove down with him and he fixed me up with a Pi Phi and a Delta Gam and I stayed at your, and George's, and eventually my, fraternity house. To tell you the truth, the college tableau looked pretty dandruffy and dull as hell to me with guys sitting around for hours in red leather chairs wearing suits and neckties and playing bridge.

Anyway, when George and I drove back to Chicago that Sunday afternoon Jackie went with us, to stay at the Armand home in Wilmette for a few days, cutting classes apparently. She sat beside me on the front seat wearing a white silk blouse and a gray skirt, I remember clearly, and I thought she was the most wise, most blasé, most appealing woman I had ever seen. Citizen from another world than mine.

That ride with her and George (he was a sleek son-of-a-bitch, too, with his pipe and his blond curls and all the jokes and French words dropped into the conversation here and there) convinced me that I must go to the university.

It never occurred to me that I (although I left the farm at age five I was still, age nineteen on the weekend I'm describing, farm oriented. The straw and horse manure were still clinging, figuratively if not literally, about my person. My costume that weekend, a green tweed jacket, green gabardine slacks, a brown-and-tan striped shirt, a red paisley tie, a broad-brimmed green felt snap-brim hat with a brown band, bright green silk socks with embroidered clocks climbing skyward, and a pair of yellowish-brown, are you listening Linda, heavy-soled shoes) even if I went to college for the rest of my days, could acquire the smooth patina of wit and erudition that I witnessed there in the car that afternoon. Without knowing my destination, however, I was determined to strike out on a route, green socks and all.

A few days earlier, my horizons had been limited to two years of commercial art school, at the end of which time, if the gods smiled, I would be able to get a high-paying job, sixty-five a week, lettering words like "Bargains,

32

bargains!" and air-brushing highlights on photographs of refrigerators. Now suddenly my horizons were infinite. I wanted, needed, burned to become a particular person, as much as possible like those two beside me. Jackie, Jackie, Jackie, crossing and uncrossing those incomparable legs and tossing her white-blonde hair back from her forehead, inhaling hungrily from her red-tipped cigarettes, swearing delightfully, and laughing like a wild violin.

I was in such a state of high fever, perspiration, damp feet and loose laughter that I wonder now how they endured my giggling presence for the several hours it took us to drive to Chicago. Were some of their quick shouts of laughter, some of the French phrases, at my expense? I have no doubt of it. But it doesn't matter now nor would it have mattered then. I was included. There was a worldly chap who spoke to me, if not as an equal, at least as a fellow human being, and a glorious, unattainable girl who owned the earth or had at least a long-term lease on it and didn't mind, apparently, my being alive on that same earth. Oh, wine in my belly!

The significant fact about Jackie is that this particular time in her life (was it a few months, a few days, or perhaps in terms of the epitome I speak of, only that afternoon) was, I think, a kind of pinnacle for her. The girl who, dramatically jilted by Armand, spent her last college year, thinner and large-eyed, as a strident leader of campus politics, was not the girl I rode to Chicago with that April Sunday.

Nor was the girl whose tense little body I used as a sexual receptacle four years later the same girl. Miserable and inturned and brutal as I had become in that time I would have had neither the courage nor the cruelty to pull the clothes off that other girl, our first private evening together, and take her roughly on the parquet floor of her sister's dining room.

I treated her, in our short time together, carelessly, coldly, humiliatingly, not only because I was at that time capable of such treatment but because at that time, and perhaps from then on, she pleaded for such treatment. She sought me out in restaurants, in the streets, in my bed, because she crazily needed to weep, not for her indignities, her shame, or her bruised body, but for George Armand. Still for him.

I nibbled at that ill-tasting truth for a long time and when I finally swallowed it whole I called her on the telephone one mid-afternoon and invited her for cocktails at five-thirty. I had never invited her anywhere before.

We sat down, there was no effort by now at smiling or being nice, and ordered drinks. After the waiter brought them and moved away I said, "I don't think there's anything I can do for you anymore except maybe kill you and I don't want to do that. I like you too much and I like myself too much."

She sat looking at me for a moment, then she said, "You are really a self-centered pain in the ass," and got up and walked slowly out of the place, nevermore to return. I finished her drink and my own, left the waiter a tremendous (as I recall) gratuity and strolled home along Lake Shore Drive.

As I mentioned earlier, I seem to have a spidery memory that you stepped into the breach at this point so you have undoubtedly heard her biography of me in all keys and all colors. So be it. Let the masochists and sadists who attend them rest in peace.

The grass blades rise slowly
After each footstep
The wounds go on throbbing
After the guns stop.
                    – Millard Hofer
(composed on a menu while drunk in Stuttgart)

CHAPTER NINE

Do you imagine that I was unfaithful to Linda when we were married? Most people who knew us and who know me assume that, I guess. After Gregg was born and Linda was just home from the hospital, my mother who had come cross country for the birthing (Lawdy, Miss Scarlett, I don't know nuthin' 'bout birthin' babies) said to her one afternoon when they were alone (I was out on some dusty location, playing cowboy), "You be careful, honey, not to get in a family way now for a while. You get your figure back and look pretty again. When you're all swollen up and out of shape, that's when those actresses move in."

Linda thought that advice was very funny. I was never sure, nor am I to this moment, whether she trusted me completely or just didn't give a good God-damn. I guess she trusted me. She should have. I never slipped, not once, when we were married. Even in the two years when we were keeping company or walking out together (excellent expression) before we were married, much of which time we were separated – she in New York, me in California – even then, bound as I was by nothing but conscience, I played it almost straight. Only minor incidents, fast and furious and against my pace.

There were two actresses (turn up the volume, sweet mother of mine), one a drunk, the other a virgin. The drunk spent the entire night (I finally fled in sleepless desperation at four a.m.) in a derlirium-tremen (but phony) type demonstration that bored me and kept me raw-nerved and awake long after her pelvic irritation, and mine, had been soothed.

The virgin, caught on the *poignard* of wanting to grab and hold and give and take everything in sight and at the same time somehow retain the invaluable membrane, worth a million dollars or thirty cents depending on your viewpoint, between her legs, ended up hysterical, violated and sated at last in every conceivable way other than the obvious. But smug in the knowledge that she had turned me into a limp rag. And miracle of the age, membrane still intact.

Then there was Birdie Gold (top that!) whom I had met in New York the first day I got off the boat from Europe. There is a long, involved, and tragic (perhaps I'm wrong) story about her that will not be told now. Or ever perhaps. When I arrived in Los Angeles the first time (more than two years after I'd met Birdie and nearly six months after our saying goodbye for what we thought was the last time, sitting in Longchamps at Madison and Fifty-fifth, I told her about Linda and me and she cried a little, said all right, and flew out to California to become the mistress of Stan Gold who had divorced her a month before in Mexico because of me. "Why'd you have to pick *him*, the goy bastard?") she showed up at the Knickerbocker Hotel one afternoon (she'd read in the *Hollywood Reporter* that I was in town), dropped her sweet summer clothes like flowers inside my door and said, "Fuck me good, honey. I think I can get pregnant today."

The next morning she called and said she hadn't told me the day before but she was living with Stan again and she was afraid of what he might do if he found out about us. So she didn't think she'd better see me any more.

Keep in mind that all this happened before Linda and I were married. Two or three years later, married long since, we were driving along Olympic Boulevard in my juiced-up white convertible with the top down and Gregg sitting beside us in his baby car-seat with its own steering wheel and gear shift. Birdie pulled up beside us at a stop light. Another woman and several kids were in the car with her. She looked over at me and I said, "Hi, Birdie," and she took a big drag on her cigarette, sucking in her cheeks the way she always did, took a long look at Linda and Gregg, and said, "Hello." The light changed then and she beat me away from the intersection. I let her.

"Who's that?" Linda asked and I said, "Some idiot girl I met once in New York." "She sure looked at me funny," Linda said. "She looks at everybody funny," I said.

Also, after I started with Linda but before we were married, there was Dort. Nothing serious. Just friends. She was married and had a lover. I was not married but serious about Linda ("God, she's so *young*," Dort said. "Revolting.") and anything that had ever flowered for us was long since pressed between the leaves of a book. Still, however, we continued to take pleasure (periphrasis) from each other. Dort (I say this with all respect for her warmth, generosity, and the admirable tilt to her pelvis) did not have a really good liaison system between her vital centers. She believed, I think, that sex is something it is not and conversely she refused to believe that it is simply and rewardingly what it is. I suspect that she can't quite, in the sense that I hold dear, make it.

Quand-même, I have no complaint. Our Hollywood days, as opposed to the tortured, raw-hearted Chicago time, the involved New York weekends, or the humid two weeks in Paris were friendly, matter of fact, and smiling. And laughing. If making love doesn't bring you to crazy laughter, then you've got the wrong woman or you're doing it wrong.

Dort and I didn't sleep together or even go to bed in those Hollywood days. Never time for that. "Hairdresser in half an hour, darling," or "I'm meeting the Greek at The Beachcomber at four." She rarely took off her dress. She sat gracefully, black-haired, blue-eyed, sun-tanned, on the kitchen table or on a kitchen chair, hoisted her skirt around her waist, closed her eyes, tightened her earrings, held out her arms and said, "Darling."

I miss Dort. Not the way she is now but the way she used to be. But miss her or no, like her or no, pelvis tilted or no, I never touched her after Linda and I were married.

There once was a boy who set out on his way to
   the city
He wandered and waited and finally came to the city.
There once was a boy who was destined to die in
   the city
And destiny followed the boy on his way to the city.
The boy and the city, tra-la, tra-la
The beautiful city, tra-lickety-la.

Why go to such lengths to document my fidelity to Linda? What pangs of guilt could be behind such a process? None, I think. None, I'm convinced. Or at least none I sincerely hope.

CHAPTER TEN

Does all this, does *any* of this, bridge the fifteen-odd years since you and I have seen each other? Not counting those two evenings plus the afternoon ceremony that week in your city. I'm sure it doesn't. And I know no solid reason why it should. I'm against digging up old friendships, old loves, old washing-machine motors and the like. On the other hand, though I have few friends, nearly none, friendship is valuable to me. If it were less valuable, perhaps I would have more friends.

What about *our* friendship? Close? Not in college. In Chicago those few months when you were testing your wings and your patience on that financial paper? Not really close then either. When then? Never, perhaps. So where's the link? What about the bird that flies backward because he doesn't care where he's going but damn well wants to know where he's been? You think I'm going to draw some conclusion? You're mistaken. We sell dreams here, party favors, artifacts and comic greeting cards for all occasions. I'm wandering around picking up fuzz from flying pigeons, feathers from feeding gulls (you know why and I know why too, of course, but I don't want to dwell on it) and when I get through I'm going to make a soft pillow, an orange one, perhaps. Then I'll lay my head on it, yawn twice, smile up at the ceiling, and put a neat blue hole in my right temple (I'm righthanded).

Don't be disappointed because I said we weren't close friends. You are, *enfin*, my intellectual conscience, ex best man (I do not hold that against you) and most important I am genuinely and profoundly attracted to your wife.

Linda and I had a fine time in your city after we bandaged the wedding-night wounds. *My* wounds. She wasn't disturbed, thought it was just a silly rift. Four days we stayed there after the wedding.

She put in quite a few hours in department stores or staring into their windows and we had a few words about that. One day, late afternoon, cold sober and sore-footed, I remarked that I sometimes got the impression that the only things of value in her life were things that could be looked at, handled, and purchased in stores. She, also cold sober and sore-footed, defended herself hotly. As so often happened afterward, she missed the point of my remark and defended the wrong case. She assumed (good, practical, French-Canadian stock) that I was talking about money. Afraid she would spend too much. Since I had no desire to win or even to appear in court for *that* litigation, I let her wrap up the judge, the jury, and public opinion, accepted my sentence without tears, and meekly window-shopped with her for three hours the next morning. At lunch she said triumphantly, "*See*, I didn't buy a thing." I said, "You're a very good girl."

In retrospect I have to admit to myself it was a well-marked highway. And not just in retrospect, either. *Then*. Little things. Bitchy little things. And you say to yourself, "Oh, come on, for Christ's sake, let's be big about it. How can a silly thing like that *matter*?" But it did matter enough for me to wonder, several different times, if this is as great as it's cracked up to be, would she do this or would I do that? And the head always came up with the same answer. Or what time seems to indicate was the right answer. "Have fun, be sweet," I told myself, "but remember she's a child. Her motives and emotions are half-formed and subject to the gusts of the future. Be wise, old redhead. Remember, you've traveled this route before. You are a professional girl appreciator, an experienced evaluator. *Doucement!*"

> Wurra, wurra –
> Lackaday –
> Why dig it up?
> I have to.

In another sense, I'm making a fundamental error when I interpret everything that went before in terms of what happened ultimately. At least I prefer to believe that. Any other conclusion leaves me with a distorted and unrecognizable picture of myself. I need to feel that Linda and I had something that was good – at some time we must have. Something, in some way, surely had some kind of half-assed value. But I can't describe it or remember it. Not for the life of me. All I can do is try to keep moving. Try to make things better than they were. Try to piece together some kind of answer for myself, some way of living without my kids.

CHAPTER ELEVEN

While I was looming my fabric of fidelity, what was apple-cheeked Linda up to? I honestly believe that's none of my business. "But she was your wife," (as you damn well know, having been there at the altar for the kill) say the legions at the gates of the town. In reply, silencing them with a gesture, I say, "Maybe."

I'm sure I was her husband. Whether she was my wife in an absolute sense (the only worthwhile one) is something that only she knows. In view of the fuzzy circumstances surrounding our brisk divorce, etcetera, etcetera, one would tend to suspect that she was less my wife, perhaps, than I would have liked her to be, or believed her to be, or would have liked to believe her to be. Here again, however, there's no way of knowing. And if I don't know, how can I care? The fact is I care about everything. I can't help it.

What we arrive at, my intellectual friend (two things I remember from your infrequent letters, three or four at the most, when I was in Europe. One . . . "I find the world holds no carrots for me." And two . . . "If I don't change my way of living, an eastbound express train will soon list my head on its timetable") is this: My fidelity was not just to Linda but to myself or perhaps my image of myself or one step further – to my image of myself as husband.

Is this wrong? Is it cerebral and anti-visceral and completely apart from that blessed if tortured, state which we refer to as (though I cherish the condition, I abhor the scabby, calloused, frayed, maligned and stained word) love? I don't think so. God, I *can't* think so. Mustn't I live in terms of my standards just as I walk in terms of my skeleton? If not, then I've really spent all these years harvesting broken glass.

Recess time. Buckle your galoshes, muffle your fragile throat, snap your mittens (lined with rabbit fur) and be very careful on the monkey bars.

Headstone: Here lies the major work (himself) of a minor artist.

CHAPTER TWELVE

This morning I slid from a bed of sin (marvelous) at seven-fifteen, showered, shaved, and breakfasted on a cold hamburger patty (heavy with garlic – cooked last night), an avocado with Italian dressing, a piece of hard-as-stone but delicious chocolate cake from Babka around the corner and a delicate crystal glass of Drambuie. Then I kissed still-in-bed Alicia and frosty-breathed (fifteen degrees here today) my way to the subway, to Fordham Road, and the wet-mouthed, sticky-cheeked love of my two kids. Then a wretched cup of coffee. Linda put sugar in it although I have never taken sugar in my coffee and she fixed my coffee every morning for five years. Does that signify anything, doctor?

Excerpt from an old letter from Hofer:

I would like to see and expect to see a noval that gestates from a speck of living matter, spreading in concentric and overlapping circles to some edge, undertowing back to the center point and mixing and spreading out again. Not a story or a tale or a theatre-piece with an exposition added. Not a well-made example of word-architecture, planned and plotted or pushed and prodded and squeezed into peaks and hollows. With rests and climaxes and denouements, conflicts and resolutions. These are considerations after the fact.

The fact is *art*. And art is what artists do. Nothing else, analyzed, planned, controlled, or crappily handi-crafted, ever.

Another day. It's snowing this morning, fine and cold and driving. But not so cold as yesterday. Twenty-seven degrees, the Madison Avenue thermometer kept flash-ing as I walked the sixteen blocks from Alicia's apart-ment (leaving her fluffed and tumbled still in the warm bed – it's Saturday today and she doesn't go to work; she doesn't like me to leave her on Saturdays because there's really nothing for her to do by herself – she doesn't have that gift – but I have to go, so I go.) to Luther's place (dark and cloistered and silent and to enter it, for a solitary ape like me, is like skip-ping through a secret door to ultimate peace) on Fifty-eighth Street.

Luther comes home from France in twenty days and then I'll be back in some grim hotel or other unless Mrs. Brokaw, queen of the cold-water flat realtors, finds a hole for me to crawl into that I can afford and stomach. I could move in with Alicia but I like her too much to inflict myself on her, willing though she may be or willing though she may imagine herself to be.

I'm blessed, you know. I'm never lonely. Frustrated, nervous, angry, suicidal even, but never lonely. There may, of course, be loneliness there in the frustration, the nervousness, or the anger but by and large I have no aching need for the presence of my fellows. On the other hand there were many days during those last months in Paris when I fled regularly from my room to a café downstairs. This, however, I have concluded, was done to escape myself rather than to seek out others. Or do I deceive myself altogether? Is this, perhaps, the true nature

46

of loneliness, a screeching need to lose oneself, if only for a while?

Last night I dreamed about J.J. Sixteen years since I've seen her. Seventeen years, really. When I saw her the last time but one in that town in Minnesota where she was teaching drawing our first year out of university I had already met Dort in Chicago. You were there and you know the lightning burns I was suffering and enjoying then. J.J. knew it, too. She didn't know details or names but she knew something had blown it out for us. She tried to laugh it away but she cried instead. She hated to cry. I felt nothing. Just a pull back toward Chicago and the electrical storm. Later, it was different. I felt terrible. Not for J.J. but for myself. I still feel rotten about that whole time and those careless decisions. I am careful now not to dwell on that time. Not that J.J. was the final answer. There were lots of things against us, against our going on together and living in Fond du Lac and me selling insurance for her father and all the rest of it. But those things didn't swing the pendulum. Dort did. That's what disturbs me. It was the first clear, isolated moment in my life when I held gold in one hand and horse-shit in the other and threw away the gold. I'd like to say it was the last time, but it wasn't. The last time was probably yesterday but I won't know that until tomorrow. And day after tomorrow I'll know about today's ratty decisions. And two days after I die perhaps I'll know how I could have avoided that.

The dream about J.J.: I was somewhere, in my parent's home, I expect, and I was sitting in a chair with J.J. on my lap and lots of relatives standing around smiling and clasping their hands and clucking to each other. It was not a sensual dream. There had been a sensual passage earlier but I'm not sure that it was J.J. on the bed and it's not important anyway. In the dream I said something clever to her like where have you been all these years and she leaned her head on my shoulder and said she was still in Fond du Lac. "I'm librarian for the opera company there." The opera company? In Fond du Lac? She'd never married, of course, in the dream and the implication was clear, as the closing music crept in, that we (both of us still bright-eyed, slim, and unlined) would go on together, hand in hand and all that orange-blossom crap.

The fact of the matter is that she's happily married to a guy who owns a distillery in Louisville, they have eighty-seven golden-haired children (all under ten), and they play golf and drink planter's punch in the summer, then swoop down to Daytona Beach in the winter, and they don't need me for a second for any purpose whatsoever.

Loyal friend that you are and a sick romantic (why else your Hamlet obsession?) I'm sure you're saying to yourself if not to me, "Yeah, but don't think for a minute that she doesn't wonder, too, how it might have been. You've had an exciting life and traveled all over and she must have heard about all that or read about you in the papers. I'm sure she thinks it might have been a great, fine life with you."

Not true. The very last time I saw her, my last spring in Chicago before I went to Europe, three years after we, she and I, had graduated and nearly two years after our last previous meeting (see above) in Minnesota, she called me one morning at the office and said, guess who's in town, and we had lunch together.

She was married by then (I knew it, thanks to alumni magazine and one of her sorority sisters who had made sure I wasn't left with the impression that J.J., one of their best girls, was going to sit around gathering moss

48

and waiting for a red-haired hick like me to make up his mind) and pregnant.

At lunch I played young executive and she played young matron. We were both bad in the roles but still it was good to see her and be with her again.

I asked her after lunch if she'd like to go up to my place and see my new paintings. I had won an oil-painting prize in Detroit and had exhibited two years in a row at the Chicago Art Institute and I thought I was pretty hot and important stuff. But she said no, thanks. "I can't stand that depressing place you live in."

So we walked a few blocks along the lake and then I put her in a cab and sent her back to her daddy bourbon man. (Actually, he's a handsome, athletic chap with hair on his chest, nice white sneakers, a tennis racket, and all the rest of it. Plus money. I met him one summer at the Fond du Lac Country Club when he was *out* wanting in and I was *in* wanting out.) She shook my hand and I kissed her freckled cheek (what sweet souvenirs) and we said goodbye; she had a strange expression in her eyes.

As the cab rolled away I had one of my flashes of insight. She had come to see me, and she had undoubtedly discussed it beforehand with Mr. Bourbon, to reassure herself it was all over, to shore herself up, to find out once and for all whether she had made the blue-ribbon choice. And as sure as there's fire at the center of the earth, when she looked at me just before getting into the taxi, a voice inside her was saying, "Thank God I didn't marry *him*."

I'm sure she went back to her husband, embraced him gratefully, and was an adoring, excellent wife for six months or a year or perhaps from then on.

My unhinged imagination, you murmur. No, dear friend. I know that feminine figure eight as well as

49

I know my pocket. A key word or gesture, properly timed, can push the boulder over the edge and make the girl, the woman, the bewildered child feel compassion or pity, if only for a moment, for me. That's all that's required. She is free then to go back to her husband or her father, whoever helps her to feel pity for *herself*. Thus she becomes, by some perverse formula, *whole* again. Think it over, logician.

CHAPTER THIRTEEN

Linda: Meeting you (meaning me) and marrying you were
the best things that ever happened to me. The
things you talk about, the things that interest you,
the things you do, are all so new and wonderful
to me. I didn't know such things existed. I'm so
happy, Jim. I'm going to be such a good wife to
you and I'm going to make you very happy. You'll
see.

Linda: (five years later): The trouble with you is, you
think you're God. You and your theories and your
big mouth. You're just a phony and a bully and
I don't know what I ever saw in you in the first
place. You're a big nothing.

Me: I don't think I'm God. I only suspect I'm God. I
only *want* to *be* God. What's wrong with that? At
least you can't accuse me of not being ambitious.
You show me the real God, or even his picture,
and I'll stop being God. Until then, I'm the only
God there is.

Linda: Very amusing. Sick, but really very funny. Always
with the words. You are very slick with the words,
Jimbo! You can always twist things around and
make me look like a crumb, you and your big
college education. Does that make you a hero?
Not a chance. I'd rather have a heart. At least *I*

have a heart. I have some feelings. All you have are words and theories and sarcasm and your big mouth. What a fool I was. You had me thinking you were Albert Schweitzer.

Me: Albert Schweitzer?

Linda: Yes, him or some kind of superior person. Well, you're not superior to anybody. You just think you're superior. You talk as though you were going to change the world but you can't even – you can't even screw in a light bulb. Big mouth! Big *mouth*!

Me: I'd appreciate it if you'd try not to wake the children.

Linda: Why not? Let's get them up. They know you're a phony. Or they *will* know it soon enough. Everybody knows it except you. And you probably know it too. You just won't admit it.

Me: Look, Linda. Since you're loaded . . .

Linda: Who's loaded?

Me: . . . and not making any sense, I guess I might as well go out.

Linda: Go ahead. Who cares? *Go* out. At least I won't have to fix your dinner.

The people I have met here in New York these last weeks who knew Linda and me together always say, "We were so surprised. What went wrong?" And I, smooth, imperturbable creature – hair combed, features in place, standing on a cold corner in my grey cashmere muffler, bought at Marshall Fields in Chicago when Linda and I, freshly wed, were on our way to Missouri for Christmas with my family, or in my green plaid cashmere muffler, gift from Alicia, or inside, sipping from a tall scotch and water or rum-on-the-rocks (Mexico and hot sand and Helen on the cool tile floor) have heard myself saying the same phrases over and over. "It was a basic conflict of values." That's what I decided to say at first and I did for a while, switching only when I got tired of looking at the confused faces.

Or "The old story – oil and water." This makes for even more confused faces but I like the enigmatic quality of it and I still say that, more often than anything else.

Some of the other recurring lines are, "Ah, yes, *she* wanted it. I would never have divorced her. Don't believe in divorce when there are children involved." Or, slight variation on the above, "We both needed to be apart, but I would never have suggested divorce. Because of the children. I'm old-fashioned about that."

Most Mount Olympus of all. "I don't think anything *goes* wrong with marriages, do you? They end badly, it seems to me, because they start badly."

And for the really persistently curious, these other tattered statements: "She had no grounds for divorce, but a legal separation, on the other hand, is easy to get; and since a separation would have kept me from living with the children, I saw no reason to play dog-in-the-manger about a divorce." And, "Of course it's a pity about the kids but there was nothing I could do."

There, of course, is the edge of the razor. Although I know in all honesty there really *was* nothing I could do, still, nagging and whining inside me these last months is a persistent troll voice suggesting that there was perhaps some unnamed something I might possibly have done. But screw it, every moment has its own dimensions and those moments, for me, for Linda, for the children, and for anybody else who wants to draw cards, are past. My fatherhood consists now of weekly checks in the mail to mommy (made out to her new name) and trips to Fordham Road to visit, play games, and read from the A.B.C. book.

If it sounds as though the whole situation is barbed-wire painful to me, if it sounds as though I'm profoundly sorry, that is correct. The sorrow, however, is not for myself. It's not for any person, really, not even for the kids. It's just a stumbling, aching, unfinished kind of empty feeling that I get when I see something or somebody wasted, when shoots that gave promise of growing and blooming turn earthward suddenly and shrivel up.

I gave up on Linda some time ago. The children I gave up, at least a large part of them, when I agreed at last to the divorce. But the idea of myself as husband and father, good or bad, I cannot shuck; the concept of the family unit can't be easily pushed away.

My lawyer said, "In six months, you'll thank me." It's less than six months and I *do* thank him. My parents, agonized by their concern for the children but surprisingly loyal and sympathetic to me, said, "You're like a different person since the divorce. You're sweet and yourself again," when I took the boys there (I have them for weekends and all holidays) for Christmas.

I nod and smile and soberly agree with people who wish me well, but inside the contradiction lives, rustles about, and dusts pollen. It's one thing to realize at last that you've chosen badly. The attempt to figure out *why* it happened, *how* the choice was made, is quite another matter. Who am I? *Where* am I? Where in Hell am I going?

CHAPTER FOURTEEN

Enough about you. Let's talk about me for a while. I am not a profligate, a professional fornicator, a pimp (although there were those in Paris, I learned with pride, who thought this of me) or a member of any other interest group that cleaves inordinately to females. Nonetheless I am delighted to say that there is no apartment, no street, no song, no painting, no season of my life that, brought to mind, does not bring with it at once the face, the voice, the presence of a woman, *the* girl of that time.

If it were said of me that I am the sum of the women I have known (it has *not* been said, to my knowledge) should I be disheartened by such a remark? I think not. Shouldn't I feel warmth, take pride in, a person who has chosen me, inspired me, held me? Of course I should. I love women. The lesser ones and the crazy, nutty, boring, irresponsible, selfish actions that occasionally spring from the noblest ones in no way diminish the soft-eyed, doe-skinned group itself. I have never stopped loving any girl I have loved. I don't understand a love that stops. I don't *believe* that love. I love Linda as I always have. Not as she would have had me love her and not perhaps as I would have wished to love her. But I love her all the same. I cannot fault her without seeing my own face and head on her shoulders. When I feel the need to exonerate myself, to make myself shining and blameless, I can do it. But it's Linda's face, then, I find on my skull. Not my own. The mixture as before. The ripples circle away from the dropped stone and for each one that goes out, one comes back to meet it.

CHAPTER FIFTEEN

The boys spent several hours with me today. Hot-shot Arthur, age three next week, confidence man, comedian and future mass seducer of girls, came first. Gregg had gone with Linda for his weekly hour of speech correction (I think he talks great; he's barely four years old for Christ's sake) but he showed up in time to watch a pre-lunch cartoon program on television.

Linda, who'd had some catastrophe with her hair, spent hectic minutes in the bathroom teasing and bullying it back into the desired chaos. Then she machine-gunned out on her spike heels bound for a luncheon engagement. She stopped at the door, she's very insecure, poor thing, and said, "I look terrible today for some reason. How do I look?"

I have never found fault with her appearance (Your problems are not physical, I used to say to her in the light-hearted moments of our heavy-hearted liaison. She found the statement elliptical and not funny) and if I did I wouldn't hint of it to her, knowing that her whole foundation in this life rests specifically on the face that looks back at her from the mirror. So I said, "You look all right to me." "But I don't really look too great, do I?" "You look fine," I said, and she said, "you're no help." Then she triggered the machine gun again and away she went. Out the door to her star-spangled destiny.

At twelve-thirty or shortly after, I turned back the rug in the bedroom. There's no dining room, the kitchen's small, and I don't want to spot Luther's nice red living-room carpet. I set up a card table at the foot of the bed, hauled the two vaqueros from in front of the television screen and set them down to a luncheon of cottage cheese and fruit, a glass of milk (Gregg also drank the syrup from the peach can. Arthur "can't yike it.") and one butterscotch Life Saver each.

I sat at the table with them with a large mug of milk (Don't you yike coffee, Daddy? It's good for you – I like it all right but it's not particularly good for you – Mommy drinks coffee – I know she does but that doesn't mean it's good for her – How about cigarettes? – They're not good for you either – Mommy smokes cigarettes – I know she does but they're not good for her – How about candy cigarettes? – They're better for you than real cigarettes – I yike candy cigarettes) and a pickle and pimento loaf (special this week at Safeway) sandwich on whole wheat.

After lunch we gathered round the toilet bowl (a big treat for the boys) and relieved ourselves in unison. (You have a big one, don't you, Daddy? – Yes, compared to yours – I need a big one, don't I? – Uh-huh, if you say so.)

The boys crawled into bed then and slept from one-thirty till three and I slept from one thirty till two. After three, I got them up and dressed them and they stood around on one leg waiting for Mommy.

About four o'clock she arrived. She hit the bathroom again as soon as she came in and then she asked for three aspirin. Headaches for weeks now, she said. She'd been to the doctor after lunch. "You'd better give up that bone-cracker and go to a real doctor," I said, making pointed allusion to the chiropractor quack who had been

58

an integral part of our separation, having assured her that he would testify that her life with me was turning her into a nervous wreck. Nervous she was and is but any assumption that this condition triggers from me seems a shaky hypothesis.

Anyway, I put my hands on her shoulders this afternoon, kissed her on the forehead, first time I've touched her in months, and said, "You do look like hell. What's the matter?" and she said, "I don't know."

That type of scene I am anxious to avoid. I don't believe in tender relationships between divorced idiots and even if I did, I wouldn't believe in it in our case. You're either married or you ain't and we ain't. At the same time, however, I don't want her to fool around and die and she would be just disorganized and corny enough to do something like that.

Yeats wrote a dandy epitaph for himself:

> Cast a cold eye on life, on death
> Horseman, pass by.

Today, more specifically in the last hour, for the first time since all the madness with Linda began and certainly for the first time since the divorce three and a half months ago, I feel that I'm beginning to dig out. It's a God-damned hell of a terrific feeling if I can just make it stick or, failing that, remember which button to press to make the feeling come back.

CHAPTER SIXTEEN

I worked on a construction gang (we were building a factory, biggest aluminum extrusion plant in the world) with a man, snag-toothed, leather-skinned (he looked very old to me then – he was probably forty) who came from the Arkansas hills and like most construction workers had that business in his blood as surely as a freight switchman or a carnival roustabout has his unlikely, gritty trade deep-welled in his veins. Its appeal to him was clear and specific, "Summer work. Ah only work in the summer. Spend the entire winter in a shack on the White River, fishin' and fuckin'."

Ugly, illiterate and inarticulate, he had a solid reputation among his fellow shovelers, concrete puddlers, form-suckers, wheelbarrow jockeys et al, as a cocksman. He was banned, however, from the local whorehouse on a complaint to the madam from one of her front-line girls who whined, "He lak tuh et me up!" As often as three or four times a day, never less than once – at lunch hour, he would wink one black-button eye and say, "Ah nevah pass one up. Always scared ah'll miss a good un!"

Bless you, sun-blackened, weather-lined, snuff-dribbling knight of the White River! May your summers be easy, your banishments from tenderness brief, and your winters long.

After that back-breaking summer, age twenty-one,

carrying railroad ties soaked in creosote, I vowed never to do physical labor again. Didn't. Cut to age twenty-four. Upon leaving the furniture business in Chicago I made a second vow. Never to do *any* kind of labor again. Didn't. Cut to the present. Yesterday I made a third vow. "I will not starve this winter." Problem – how to avoid it.

"But," he said, laughing gaily and scratching himself discreetly, "there are flaws in all gems, follies in all flings, risks in all ventures. What am I but a cork a-bobbing? What difference whether I sink now or with the next wave? What does it matter, in the perspective of centuries, whether the evening tide finds me still floating or no?" It matters to me, by God.

Let's get on with it. Exorcised, flagellated, purified. I feel new marrow in the bones, new juice in the juicer, new spring in the faltering, flat-footed step, new and excellent eighty-proof sweat in the glands. New glands, I daresay. Oh yes, oh yes, oh yes, my friend! The piss and vinegar returneth!

I was a premature baby. Seven months. In moments of depression, I've often wondered what securities, what benefits that two extra months in the womb might have given me. "You show promise, young man, so we're going to skip you from second grade to the last year of graduate school."

In periods of high confidence, I assure myself that premature birth was an indication of my driving direction (I will not be denied). All the same, nine months minus two is a big subtraction. Does it mean that I'll live twenty-two percent longer or for a twenty-two percent shorter time? Will I be fulfilled one hundred and twenty-two percent or will I never achieve more than seventy-eight percent of myself?

I tell you this story not to give you cause for philosophical reflection but to prod you to say to Gwen, "Isn't it incredible that Tyler started life so weakly, so tentatively, so puny and ugly, and he has nonetheless become the glorious creature we love so well. Tall, handsome, brilliant, responsible, talented, loving, thoughtful, destined for greatness. Marvelous! And to think he's *our* friend."

CHAPTER SEVENTEEN

Dave and me, big, disjointed, cerebral, sweet-natured, too-early-matured Dave, swinging down through Terre Haute and Springfield, Missouri (sleeping in a strange parked car there – Dave even put on pajamas, just like a fucking hotel) and Oklahoma City and Norman and on down through the inexhaustible, boring and empty, dogs howling in the night, length of that back lot called Texas. And on down, then, through Laredo, Nuevo Laredo, Monterey, Tampico (nobody there but us lost souls, the concrete walls of the hotel smelling and feeling to your hand like they'd just shucked the forms off the day before) and over and down and around to Mexico City with me throwing up, not everywhere, but almost everywhere. And Chilpancingo and Taxco and (Helen, Helen, Helen) Acapulco.

Helen, sweet Jesus, the only perfect love. She died to keep it perfect. Never, you fool. Nonetheless, her dying kept it perfect like a never-ending liebestode. (The romantic, drooling, unreal bastards are overrunning the world. With me, red-haired, freckle-armed, broken-field runner, pigskin tucked in the crook of the elbow, in the thundering, sod-shredding lead.)

No one but me knows that what we found and planted and nurtured and harvested and fed on was gossamer and delicate, pale as tequila. But oh what a kick, what a glow from tequila, my friend. What nourishing fire in the bones, what hangover-free, three-dimensional wonder. No one knows but me that caged in my tomb-room in Chicago or even in her sun-lighted, grass-bordered, lemon tree-scented hacienda (gift from her in-laws) in Inglewood, we'd have stomped and pounded and danced the juice from the grapes and guzzled and slurped and bolted the wine in short order.

But no matter what inevitably, painfully, might have happened, it didn't happen, Lord. When Dave told me that fall in Chicago that she was dead, that she'd gone to the desert with her husband on his furlough and caught pneumonia and died in one day, I knew I'd never see the dreary end of it because the dreariness had been avoided by its ending in the high-tide, sweet-smelling middle ("Oh, how I'll miss you, you redheaded son of a bitch") with the sand barely brushed from our hair, the Mexican freckles still brown on our backs, our noses, our ear shells. And the taste of the salt, of the rum, of her mouth, still fresh on my lips.

Helen's dead, Dave said. He wanted to hurt me, I think, because he thought I had treated her carelessly, that I didn't see her sweetness, or seeing it, didn't let her know I saw it.

What a fool he was. I gave her pound for pound of all the sweetness I received and she, with that blood-red sensual flower in her hair would, if she could hear me, shout and laugh and sing in support of this.

I knew her. I *was* her and she was me. And Dave, even if he knew this, didn't know it enough. He didn't know we were lost and floating and wanting it that way. And at the same instant reaching for some personal branch to hang on to when the weather would turn quickly and permanently bad, when the sweetness would leave and finally, when everything would be gone. Dave didn't understand. If he had, he wouldn't have tried to hurt me when he told me she was dead.

CHAPTER EIGHTEEN

All the previous spring we had talked about our trip, Dave and I. At first nobody believed in it and maybe we didn't believe in it all the way ourselves. Dave did, though, I'm sure, because he'd always had a wild hair plus a family with money and a willingness to let that hair grow as wild as he willed it.

When he finished high school, precocious and high-strung and sixteen years old and a champion barefoot high jumper, his father suggested three colleges to him and made arrangements for him to visit each one so he could decide where his future lay. "None of them," Dave said when he came home.

His father suggested he look further, on his own, and he did, driving in a Ford roadster back and forth, up and down through the country for fifteen months. Winding around, stopping, lingering, and visiting schools.

Then, as if to assure his father that his wandering months had brought him wisdom and maturity, he selected at last our school, the one his father had plumped for, mildly but specifically, and one of the three universities Dave had visited first a year before.

The war was still going on that four-years-later spring, petering out but still shooting, and I, already discharged, and Dave, strong as a hay hand but somehow not draftable, became close friends – because most of our other friends (you, for example) were gone. Much of the time when I was not with Dolly Corso (that was our epoch), tending furnaces, studying, or waiting tables, I was with Dave.

Patterns were shattered that year. Fraternities were closed or filled with girls (dwell on that a moment), officers' training candidates marched back and forth, jeering at me for being a draft dodger (as I walked hand in hand with bulging Dolly) not realizing that I had fought bravely the battles of Fort Thomas, Kentucky, and Randolph Field; Dave lived in an apartment next door to the Phi Psi house, and I was pigging it, working for my room, as usual, in a dark-shuttered cell behind the coffin-storage room at Twigg's Funeral Home.

Dave's original plan, much discussed that winter, was to take off, come summer, traveling light, head south through Mexico and Central America and go on until he ended up, God knew where, Dave knew less, in South America.

"I'll go with you," I said one day and Dave said, "Bungo" or some such expression he'd gleaned from Hemingway. So from then on it was *our* trip. The vicarious excitement it created bubbled all through the school and slopped over even on to the faculty. Someone in the Administration Building arranged for Dave and me to go down to Champaign and meet with the president of the university there, a meeting that seemed, when it happened, as diffuse and trackless to that grey-haired gentleman as it did to us. He mumbled over and over about his keen interest in inter-American relations, reciting gravely the names of countries and cities that are available to any moron with a map. But what bearing our stumbling journey might have on such relations he seemed at a loss, as were we, to predict.

Although we'd hitchhiked down to Champaign, it was

nearly dark when we left the president's office (because he had been able to think of nothing pertinent or even sensible to say to us, he had talked all afternoon, growing more oblique and glassy-eyed each quarter-hour) so we decided we should take a bus home.

After buying our tickets (the bus, war-time measure, was actually a twelve-seat limousine driven by a woman) and finding there would be a thirty-five minute wait, we strolled into a tavern beside the bus station. I quickly downed four beers. Dave drank three and then went beind the door marked "Caballeros." I had another beer and was turning toward "Caballeros" myself when the bus honked outside. Dave said, here we go, and I thought, what the hell, I can wait, it's only forty-five miles. So I went out and got into the bus with Dave, the lady driver, and four other females of varying ages, and away we went.

Halfway home, I knew I'd made a mistake. I would have asked for what is known in the bus business as a bush stop but the fact that the driver was a woman, that all the other passengers were women, and that the cramped bus made the situation so intimate, kept me from speaking up.

I tried several phrases in my mind. "Will you stop at the next filling station, please?" No good. She might ask why. "I'd like to make a comfort stop, please." How could a grown man say that? I was just at the edge of blurting out, "Stop the car, lady! I gotta go!" when I noticed one of the other passengers sidelong-glancing me from the seat ahead.

She was a thirtyish, brown-eyed blonde. Once I took my mind off my bladder I seemed to remember having seen her before. But I couldn't place her. We started talking and she made a few cute remarks (not as bad as "Do you think the rain'll hurt the rhubarb?" but about that vintage) and finally she said, hadn't she seen me in Castle's drug store?

Then I remembered. Without her tight white uniform and her white shoes and without her sensational, full-calfed legs in view she looked different. She was a widow, so the story went, a registered pharmacist, and she had never been known to grant any favors whatsoever to the young men of the university.

Do you remember her? You must.

Anyway, it looked as though the rose garland was perhaps going to fall on me. Or was I going to screw the whole works because of a temporary agony of the bladder? No sir. Not stout-hearted me. I simpered and grinned and tried somehow to detach myself from the pressure in my chambers.

Dave, good friend, hayseed humorist and sadistic bastard that he was, noticing my discomfort, set off on a vividly pictorial account of a trip he had once made to Niagara Falls. The torrents, the spray, the cascading currents, the mist in the air, and the deep swirling pool beneath and behind the falls. He painted such word pictures that the ladies in the bus, including the driver (she almost sideswiped an Omar bread truck) were speechless, captivated, intent on missing not one syllable. He attenuated every sentence, every watery word, every wet scene, cruelly watching my squirming all the while. He repeated and rephrased every image, projected and reprojected the whole soaking landscape so that his description lasted right up to the edge of our town. By this time, my eyes were burning so I could hardly read the city limits sign.

"Pull up here," I wheezed to the driver.

"Don'tcha want to go to the station?" she said.

"Right here," I said smiling stiffly at the pharmacist and

trying not to shout. As we pulled over and Dave opened the door, the driver said to him, "You sure have a way with words. I never heard anything described better even in a travelogue. I felt like this bus was gonna fill right up with water."

I eased myself stiffly out of the door, turned halfway to the driver and said, "Count your blessings, lady."

As the bus pulled away, I hobbled across the sidewalk, like one of the little people, unable to rise out of a crouch, leaned my head against a tulip tree and with my back to the street (my only deference to local folkways, morés, and all the rest of it), opened my fly and began the slow, painful, almost surgical emptying of my bladder, sub-bladder and all reserve tanks.

Dave stood beside me, whistling shrilly, waving one arm at the traffic and pointing his other hand in my pissing direction. "How do you feel now?" he asked when I was about halfway through my five-minute fuel transfer operation. "Go to hell, you prick," I said.

CHAPTER NINETEEN

Parenthetically, let me finish off, and quickly, the pharmacist. I saw her three days later in the drug store. I went there specifically to see her. If Dolly had known she would have poisoned me. I had enough grief with her over that tri Delt from Duluth, the one with the nutty sister upstairs at home.

Anyway, I strolled over to the pharmacist and said hello. And she said hello. I thought maybe she'd give me some help but she didn't so I said, "I'd like a small tin of aspirin, please," and she said, "Just a moment." She leaned over and fished the aspirin out of a drawer, opened the lid, tucked a slip of paper inside and said, "That will be nineteen cents."

I walked out of the drugstore and around the corner and headed back towards campus. I took the paper out of the box and looked at it. It was a printed slip with her name, address, and telephone number and the words, *Registered Pharmacist.* Underneath she had written, "Take two before bedtime. Ten-thirty?"

At ten o'clock I took Dolly home and at ten-thirty I was standing in front of the pharmacist's door, thinking it over. I knocked and she opened up with a straight face and said come in. She closed the door then and turned around and kissed me. Just an ordinary train-station kiss. No big explosion. "I'm glad you came," she said and led me into the living room.

She lived on Hazel Street about halfway out to the Deke house, on the second floor of a two-story building. Once there had been a meat market on the ground floor but now it was vacant. Her apartment must have been three or four rooms at one time but all the walls had been taken out and it looked now like one long, carpeted, over-furnished room.

She led me to a sofa and we sat down. When I glanced at the other end of the room there was a man sitting there. His hair was thick and white and he was wearing dark glasses. Most of the lamps were at our end so it was difficult to see him clearly at first. But he seemed to be sitting in a wheelchair. He coughed then, a hard, dry sound.

"That's my father," she said. "Poor thing. He's deaf and dumb. And blind now, too. And he can't get out of that chair."

"That's too bad," I whispered. "Does he stay here all the time?"

"No. He sleeps in his own room across the hall. You needn't whisper. He can't hear you."

"I see."

"He doesn't even know you're here," she said.

We sat talking for a while, she in a normal voice and I in whispers. Once in a while her father would cough and I was thinking this is a pretty nutty situation. I might as well go home and study. Suddenly there was a spasm of dry coughs from the other end of the room. It startled me. But the pharmacist just smiled and put her hand over mine. Then she leaned over against me and said, "I wish you'd kiss me."

Because you are a man of experience, I needn't describe for you the mechanics of mutual seduction – the piecemeal

72

clothes-shedding, the ponderous, trembling beginnings, the fevered mouths and cold hands. So I won't.

"Do you mind the light?" she asked.

"Well – " It wasn't just the lamp; it was noontime on the desert.

"I like it," she said and we went on. And the coughing went on.

Somehow, later (two minutes – twenty minutes?) it slowly got through to me in the hot light where I lay steaming that there was a strange, rhythmic connection between the cough spasms and the white body wrapped round mine. This beginning of something turned and tumbled in a switched-off mind, stirred and tossed and pitched up at last as a tiny glittering suspicion. Every time he coughed, she changed her position, changed her relation to me or mine to her. The more violent the cough, the quicker the adjustment. I lay there, moving, senseless as an animal, and at the same time some inner part of me rose to a perch to observe.

He coughed. It happened. He coughed again. She moved again, like a bell-trained brute. Again. Again she shifted. I rolled my eyes toward the end of the room and saw, unmistakably and chillingly, the blur of a white hand flicking something from one lens of the dark spectacles.

I stood up and pulled on my clothes. She lay back, lips parted, still quivering and watching me, silent and soft-eyed as a dog, her eyes jumping quickly then to the end of the room where the coughing had become a harsh staccato.

I kept looking at her as I backed up to the door. Then I slipped outside and closed the door softly behind me. Wanting to run, I walked slowly down the hall, then down the stairs to the street. Until I reached the sidewalk I could still hear the coughing behind me.

I walked down the street for a block or two, then crossed over and came back up the other side. I stood there half behind a tree and looked up at her windows. The shades were down. After a few minutes, her shadow showed on the shade. She was smoking a cigarette. A man stood facing her, also smoking. Then they moved away from the window.

I waited a few more minutes, then I started home. But now I ran, like a striped-assed ape. I was shivering when I got inside my room.

I called Dolly as soon as I closed the door. "Are you all right?" I said when she came to the phone. "I was asleep," she said. "Oh, I'm sorry I woke you up," I said. We said goodnight then and I closed all the shutters, locked the door, got into bed, covered up my head and said in the warm dark, "Good night, God. Thanks for everything. Good night, Dolly. I love you."

My sister, when she was in high school, had the walls of her room papered with newspaper photos of John Dillinger.

CHAPTER TWENTY

When school was out that June, Dave and I got a ride as far as Springfield, Missouri with a carload of Alpha Chis heading for New Orleans. We stopped off in Evansville to unload one of the girls and to give me twenty minutes to say goodbye to Dolly.

She had on a white silk blouse that day and she was perspiring (she had a small rib cage and toting that bosom of hers around was serious work) and she was weeping steadily. She was no more enthusiastic about the trip I was taking than my parents were. My mother, movie-orientated, said, "You go messing around down there with those greasers and somebody'll stick a machete in you."

Dolly was buckling under another burden also (in addition to my trip and her bosom). She had just graduated and I had at least two more years of school and assuming that we would be married as soon as I graduated (she assumed it, I didn't. Her father, who hated my guts, because on tiptoe he barely reached my shoulder, didn't assume it, either. "I'd rather see you an old maid than married to that redheaded bum." And there, we see perhaps his true desires.) what in hell was she going to do for the next two years? All these forces centered in her tear ducts that hot June afternoon and I had a very damp twenty minutes there in Evansville.

Poor Dolly. Last time I saw her in New York – the young Connecticut matron, suit, hat, corsage for an afternoon at the matinée, and all the rest of that crap – she had (aging or dieting) grown thin and astigmatic. But lo and behold, that ponderous, pneumatic pair of breasts would not diminish or surrender.

Dolly hated her out-of-proportion-ness. Understand-ably. As the boys on the corner used to say, chuckling and adjusting their crotches and watching the girls prance by, "They's such a thing as too much of a good thing." Dave's preference in this area, probably influenced by cereal advertising then current, "Bite-size."

Dolly solved her two-year waiting problem. I decided to work for a year in Chicago after I came back from Mexico which made our hypothetical marriage date three years away. That, coupled with her midget father's daily voodoo attacks on me, plus her learning that I had trained up from Chicago to visit with the Duluth girl (the one with the bobby-hatch sister) on a weekend when I was scheduled, in Dolly's mind, to appear at her parents' anniversary party (I suspect they weren't really married) in Evansville, plus her flipping through some letters in my desk one weekend when she was staying with me in Chicago and reading a few hot declarations from Helen which pretty well documented my Mexican summer (why in hell do girls read other people's mail anyway? Linda, had she not felt free to rifle my desk one afternoon when I was away, this before we were married, would never have known certain Swedish facts, past history, which were none of her business anyway and which eventually, I'm convinced, helped to sprinkle the grains of black powder that blasted us apart) was, in Dolly's immortal words, "Just a little bit too damned much." So she ran back to Evansville and married the first guy who said hello to her and who, coincidentally, I trust, happened to be no taller than her father.

Dave saw her a few times after she was married. He, I didn't know this until much later, was wobbly-in-love with Dolly before I started up with her. He was playing it slowly and close to the vest, not wanting to ruin his chances by moving too fast. Like a lot of sincere, well-meaning, and honorable fellows, however, he misunderstood the nature of the beast he was pursuing and didn't move fast enough.

Anyway, Dave told me Dolly's husband was a sorry specimen, a salesman of something-or-other, who collected matchbook covers and Indian-head pennies, pinched waitresses, bedded in the back seat of his car with round-heeled bar maids and street girls, wore brown socks with a blue suit, and picked his nose when he thought no one was looking.

So Dolly, who for all her faults, and they were minor, was admirably well-suited to the role of wife and home-maker and deserving of the best in the line of male solid citizens, etcetera (better than me, or certainly, *different*, at least. Papa was right about that) came up with a lemon, a brown-socked fanny-pinching nose-picker.

CHAPTER TWENTY-ONE

The summer before I met Linda, I spent six weeks in South America acting in an industrial film. When I returned to New York from Argentina, there was a message at my agent's office saying Dolly Finger had telephoned a month or so before and left a number, some exchange in Connecticut, for me to call. The name, Dolly Finger, meant nothing to me, so I didn't try the number.

Two weeks later, the switchboard girl at the agency called me one morning at a studio where I was making a toothpaste commercial (the things I do, old friend, to buy bread) and said, "Dolly Finger's after you again." She thought it was a very amusing name. I said, like where, and she said, like I've got her on the line. So I said, "What can I lose? Put her on." It was our own Dolly Corso, of course. I knew it as soon as she said hello. I said I'll buy you lunch and she said fine.

She looked good. Too thin and too-young-matron (see above) and she wore glasses all the time now. But she looked good. Also, she is a fine talker, very nourishing for the male ego, always was, so I enjoyed the lunch. I said let me know in advance when you're next in town and we'll do it again. I gave her my home number and she said she'd call.

Three days later, my phone rang. Eight-thirty a.m. I said hello and she said, "How's today? Too soon?" I said no, today was fine. I asked where she wanted to meet and she said, "Why don't I pick you up at your place? I'd like to see your paintings." Girls really say that. All the time. They do like to look at paintings, I guess.

Anyway, I said all right and gave her the address. I was living in the rat hole on Ninety-third Street then. Bathroom down the hall, hot plate in the closet. But paintings, bed, couches, etcetera as previously noted.

I strolled over to Columbus Avenue and bought some sardines and chili and crackers and beer and a bunch of other junk and when she arrived, bright-eyed behind her glasses, and bushy-tailed, and fresh off the computer train I said I thought it might be nice to have lunch here and she said, "Marvelous. Can I trust you?" and I said, "Yes, can I trust you?" and she giggled and said, "Couldn't you always, Jimbo?"

She paced around then, studying the paintings, opinionizing and theorizing and praising and trying to position me in her dimwit version of the overall history of art. I sat on the bed drinking beer, nodding my head and watching her. After about twenty minutes of the monologue she came over and sat on the edge of the bed. I undressed her and went on drinking beer while she lolled about in the manner of Rubens.

There are many women who are realistic or even pessimistic about their physical appearance but there are almost none who don't feel they look their best naked. Dolly, my remarks about her bosom notwithstanding, had a glorious golden body. Any man who criticized her proportions, observed in their naked completeness, would have to be a fool or a coward. I am a fool but not a coward.

As we sat up in bed later eating our chili, she said, "I would have died if you hadn't done that to me." And I said (cavalier of the west side, Swedish-Irish envoy to the Puerto-Rican ghetto), "Me, too."

There was a lot of loose talk then about our future relationship, ending in a nuzzling farewell in a taxi ("We must be careful") outside the railroad station. She said she'd call me the next morning and she did. She called every morning for a week as soon as Merlin Finger (or whatever the fuck his name was) had left the house to catch his train to the city.

Came a day the following week when she called and said, "I'll see you at your place at noon. Yippeeee!" (Only matrons or inexperienced girls striving for an effect say yippeee). She didn't show up. A couple of file drawers opened and closed in my head and I began to see what I suspected was a pattern. She called the next day and said she was very sorry. The car or the train or her hair or her varicose veins or some such excuse. Called every morning for another week or so. I'm dying to see you. Soon. Soon. Came the day. Yippeeee again! Didn't show up. Called next day. Apologized. I saw now very clearly what was expected of me but I waited a few more days until again she, scheduled for shipment, failed to arrive.

I stood in front of the mirror, twisted my face into a suffering mask, walked over to the telephone, picked it up, and dialed her number. It was the first time I had called her. As soon as she said hello, I said, "What are you trying to do to me?" Voice husky with grief. "Who is this?" she said. "Who *is* this?" I parroted, using ancient female device of turning words of mate against him. "That's wonderful. It's bad enough you don't show up. Now you don't even recognize my voice when I call you."

"You don't sound like yourself," she said carefully.

"I'm not myself," I groaned. "What do you expect? You're apparently very casual about all this but it's not casual for me. I let you go out of my life once and I thought I'd forgotten you. But then you came back. Voluntarily. I didn't beg you. Remember that. No matter how much I might have wanted you, I didn't beg you. You just came back, all by yourself. But now that you're back, do you expect me to pretend that nothing's happened between us? You say you'll see me and I wait and you don't show up. Do you know what agony that is? Do you? Don't play games with me. I *need* you." And so on and so on.

I finally ran down. There was silence at both ends of the wire. It was as though I could hear her shuffling through her notes. At last – clearing her throat – she began, "Please forgive me (pause) Jim, I wouldn't have hurt you like this for the world. (Wouldn't kid me, would you, sister?) I've never forgiven myself for jilting you. I know how much you loved me and I suppose I loved you, too, in a way. But the minute I met Merlin Finger (that *can't* be the bastard's name) I knew it had to be him. The reason I wanted to have lunch with you that first day was to tell you how sorry I was that I'd hurt you (uh-huh), but you seemed so cheerful and glad to see me, I couldn't bring it up. And that day at your studio (don't romantic it up, baby. It's not a studio – it's a lousy room with a sink) I don't know what possessed me. (*I* possessed you, Mrs. Finger) There's just no excuse or explanation for the way I behaved that day. Ever since then I've been trying to find a way to tell you, to explain that no matter how much it may hurt you, I can't see you again. I thought perhaps we could have a platonic friendship (Yeah? What about all those yippees?) but since you feel the way you do, I can see now that it would never work. You see, I'm very much in love with Merlin Finger (here we go again) and I wouldn't be unfair to him for anything in the world and bla, bla, bla . . ." (over and out).

Thus in the space of our short telephone conversation, she was transformed (*I* transformed her) from a disenchanted Connecticut integer (I'm giving her the best of it) who had tied her life to a slightly unsatisfactory husband (I'm really giving *that* bastard the best of it) after an unhappy love affair with a most desirable (her evaluation, not mine) young man (me), to a secure, happily married young woman whose only cross to bear in life was the realization that she had shattered the life of that young chap (me) by marrying someone else.

Not only am I content for her to have such a fantasyland impression but, as documented above, I took some pains to see that she was left with it. Altruistic? Yes, Lord! Guardian of female sensibilities? Laugh if you will, but yes.

More realistically, however, speaking of Dolly, I discovered during our naked lunch that my image of her had become inaccurate with the passing of time. In truth, her horizontal performance that day on Ninety-third Street was something less than remarkable. Barely, if I'm to be absolutely true to the facts, adequate.

On this cynical note I leave Dolly Finger (née Corso) to Heaven. Or to you – don't you wish? I leave her also to the Lower Connecticut Young Matron's Association, to the university alumni group (she's very active), to the arms of suburban lovers, itinerant brush peddlers, roofing salesmen, poll takers, Nisei gardeners, or any other male who might momentarily catch her eye.

More specifically, I leave her to Merlin Finger – may all his matchbook covers explode in his hand simultaneously!

CHAPTER TWENTY-TWO

Secret of happiness and fulfillment in this life: (attributed to many sources – I now claim it for my own) good health and a bad memory.

Army Air Corps medical records notwithstanding, I am in flagrantly good health. Blood poisoning does me in once in a while but that's so beautifully overt. Point two, as anyone in my inner circle will assure you, I am likely to sit hatted and coated in a friend's apartment for a slow pre-departure quarter-hour trying to remember the exact location of the door through which I entered. Therefore I am a happy (don't even know the word's definition, nor do I care to) and fulfilled man (never in this life or the next five or six).

Tomorrow is Arthur's birthday. Three years old. I talked with him on the telephone yesterday and made the mistake off asking him what he wanted. He recited, without pausing, what sounded like a four-page mimeographed list, passed out to acquisitive children by the toy folks. "You're too greedy," I said, "You may get nothing." He said, in a small voice, "All right, daddy-daddy," and I said (gruff papa bear), "I'll give you the rest of those butterscotch candies you left here the other day. All right?" "I yike butterscotch."

He knows, of course, in his three-year-old wisdom, that he can afford to cross stingy daddy off the donor list and still come up with a room-full of miscellany to unwrap, eat, wear, fondle, or destroy. So, this morning (I used to preach that too many toys are bad for kids. Still believe it – stopped preaching) I went to the store and bought him a fireman's hat (also one for Gregg), two books (a record for Gregg), a little yellow race car (red one for Gregg), a sheriff's badge, whistle, and keys for the jail, a gang of Civil War soldiers (both sides represented), a red ball, a big red tommy-gun (Gregg will sigh for this) and two rolls of Life Savers (two also for Gregg). In an hour or so, I'm walking over to Third Avenue to buy a small cake and three candles.

PART TWO

CHAPTER ONE

My agent telephoned this morning. I have all my mail forwarded to her since I'm a frigging Arab these days without tent, camel, or mailbox. She said there was an unemployment check there for me from the golden state or the piss-poor state (whatever they call it) of California. Fifty-five dollars. An interstate claim, it's called.

I don't object to having fifty-five dollars sent to me in an envelope, but in my present state of bankruptcy, that amount in relation to my weekly financial contributions here and there, is like putting a three-cent stamp on an elephant's ass, pushing him through the door of the post office and saying, "He's all yours, boys! Send him on to Bangkok."

The man who said every little bit helps must have been the same starry-eyed son of a bitch who said absence makes the heart grow fonder. A little bit to me is just a gnawing reminder that it ain't even close to being enough. I get drunk a couple times and Alicia gets half-drunk a couple times and we giggle and eat herring and roll around in the bed for a day or so and I'm right back where I was. Debt-ridden and destitute and sitting in a chair at her place, reading the idiotic newspaper and watching the tender creature as she strides around in her tight butter-nut slacks waiting for the knockwurst or the pot roast or the calf's liver (she guards my health, this child) to finish cooking.

Alicia hates to cook (stands in the kitchen like a prisoner) but she doesn't want me, for some reason, to know it. Nobody cooks as fast as she does or washes dishes so fast except somebody who's got to get it over with or puke. She pretends she likes to cook ("For you, darling") and I pretend that I think she likes it. So we dance along like that.

She's beginning, however, to get a cloudy look in her Spanish eye. I didn't see her for three nights this week because I was working here in Luther's apartment and dining grandly on cheese sandwiches and decaffeinated coffee. I can sense the clicking in her skull when she looks at me. "Why am I kidding myself with this one? He'll be here for two days – gone for three. Back for another day and then gone for God-knows-how-long. And first thing I know, he won't come back at all. I'll be sitting here with thirty-seven recipes for cooking knockwurst and nobody calling me anymore because I was so long putting them off for him. I should tell him to find another closet to store his summer suit and to find a new place to eat dinner. But if I suggested it, I guess he would do it. Ahhh, well, we'll see. Maybe I'll get a nice flank steak for dinner tomorrow. He looks a little pale and he likes flank steak."

Am I a mind reader? No, I'm a history student. The study of women is like the study of prize fighting. After you've fought fifty fighters, you don't run into any new types. Just variations of the first fifty. Or a combination of two or three of them maybe. A fighter, for instance, drops his left before he hooks. When you see it drop, you know he's going to hook you. You may have ten more fights before you meet another man who drops his left like that. But when one does, he's going to hook, too. You

88

watch the head, the feet, the eyes, the shoulder feints, the belly. And pretty soon, if you're smart and if you have a memory, you won't get surprised very many times. You'll get hit plenty and you won't win every match but it won't be because you're fighting wrong.

You meet a girl and you think, "She is very much like Pilar, the girl in San Sebastian." You observe her closely and sure enough she is, in many ways, not appearance necessarily, much like Pilar. So you dredge your memory and put her to a test. You say, "You're a nice girl, honey, but you must admit you're not brilliant. And you're bloody dull in bed." You watch her then. What will she do? She may laugh, she may leave, she may cry, she may slap you or she may go ahead with whatever she's doing and say, "That's why we're such a good couple, my darling."

This *new* girl, quite intelligent but unsure of her physical appeal, reacts simply and emotionally. She slaps you. *Then* she cries. What, on the other hand, did Pilar do? It was in the hotel in Hendaye the night before you were to leave for Pau on your way back to Paris. She slapped you, then she walked so slowly across the room to the window overlooking the *gare*, stood staring out for a moment, turned back then to the room and *began to cry*. Ah-ha! You see.

Of course I don't know Alicia's thoughts. But I've been down this trail before. And I've taken a few left hooks, telegraphed or not.

CHAPTER TWO

Once you can talk about yourself, the doctor said, you're well on the road to recovery. "I'm feeling much better, thank you, doctor." Recovery is something else again, but what the hell, what the hell. Recovery of what?

What about my expensive, precision-made nail clipper from the shop on Boulevard Raspail? Given to me by pudgy Erica on my God-knows-which birthday and lost apparently during last autumn's hassle when I was scrambling to get out of the apartment so Linda and the boys could move back in (one of my many mistakes). I'd certainly like to recover that nail clipper. Not for sentimental reasons but because it was an excellent instrument for clipping nails.

And how about my financial records lost in transit between California and New York – more specifically, the record of residual payments I've received in the past two years. With these in hand, perhaps, I could prevent one of our distinguished television networks from screwing me more royally than they have already.

I'd like somehow to recover the apartment I had last year in Westwood. After Linda and I had decided we would live on both coasts simultaneously; she and the children in New York (she hated California, burned to get back to New York and her foolish friends) and me there with them except for the times (often) when I had to be in orange-land-by-the-sea to play cowboys and Indians. My acceptance of this arrangement turned out to be another error in judgment on my part. "It looks like desertion," her lawyer said to her. "They could make it look like desertion," my lawyer said to me. According to Webster a definition of desertion is: The state of being forsaken by God; spiritual despondency. (Don't talk to *me*, you peri-wigged, white-hosed, bloodless sons-of-bitches about desertion.) Postscript to my lawyer: I don't mean you, good friend. The little I know of your profession makes me detest you. The little I know of you makes me admire you and detest your profession a bit less.

I'd also like to recover the red plaid shirt I left in Paris. Anna, a Polish girl who tenanted my studio there after I left wrote later – I had been in America a year by then – to a mutual friend, "If you see Jim, tell him I sold his cloths." She could have meant paint rags but I have a feeling she meant *clothes* and I have a further feeling that the shirt got peddled.

There was a camera there, too; I had expected to be back in Paris in six weeks. It's nine years now. I'm not back yet. And a file box full of important papers, including a hand-written list of all the girls I'd laid up to that time. Eight pages, single-spaced. I'm kidding. Actually, the list was written on one side of a small calling card and there was enough space left to list all the presidents of the United States up to McKinley. I'm kidding again, buddy. There wasn't *that* much space left.

Floating. That's what I'm doing. All these days since the Linda War. No matter how much I stretch my legs, the feet don't quite touch the ground. Unquiet drifting – I don't like the feeling.

The phone rang last night and it was Karin. She's a friend of Luther's and some other people I know here in New York. I ran into her last week at a party; I told her I was camping in Luther's place but that he would be back a week from Thursday and I'd have to get out. She said, "I think I have an apartment for you," and gave me a name and a phone number.

I called the man and he said he was going to California for three months, until May, and if I wanted to come look at the apartment maybe we could work out a deal. So I'll go there tonight. I expect that it will answer my needs, that we'll make a financial arrangement, and I'll have a home for three months. By that time, the floating sensation should have gone away and I'll have at least as much confidence and direction as I had at age eight. At the moment, no. But the South will rise again.

Re-tooling. That's the name of the process. The current model has either crashed or gone out of style and a new one must be designed and built. So you go through a stack of old blueprints and sepia prints and working sketches and isometrics and scale models and see what you have done in the past that may be of use to you now in your re-design, re-tooling phase. You overlook nothing because a significant change may be indicated in an old drawing or in a long-since discarded mock-up. And even if no specific comes out of this slow research, you will have gained, at least, a sense of history, a concept of your own identity as producer, a newly-braced foundation of self to use as a launching place for new work – the new model. You strip down the old production line to the bare concrete, then build it back up, piece by piece, using old tools and new tools, until gradually production can go forward again.

But screw all that, *amigo*. Let's not advertise our sincerity or exhibit unduly our high purpose lest it be held suspect in the eyes of cynics. Instead, let's cleave to the American ideal of accidental riches and instant genius. You can be rich if you'll let me be a genius. Then next week I'll be rich and you can be the genius. And when the heroin runs out, we'll both end up where we began. You – husband, father, philosopher, post-nasal dripper, lecturer, professor, lover, and sometime lecher. And I – painter, part-time Christ, denizen of furnished rooms, absentee father, cowboy actor, self-deceiver, intermittent alcoholic, collector of unemployment compensation, and relentless searcher after pussy and truth. In that order.

CHAPTER THREE

Dave and I sitting together, fourth seat back on the left-hand side, in a third-class bus from Mexico City to Acapulco. You don't want a travelogue, do you, a description of the trailside beauties? Or a social piece, detailing the physical features, the behaviourism of the Mexican nationals traveling with us? You can get all that someplace else. Besides I can't remember much about it now. Sixteen years ago. Isn't that a kick in the ass? Sixteen crazy years since Dave and I were in Mexico.

If you think we didn't cut a visual swath through that medieval Indian land, you've got it wrong. In the first place, we were the two tallest bastards between Nuevo Laredo and Guatemala City. Me six-three and Dave six-five.

We had on blue jeans and T-shirts, I had on an army field jacket (later sold in Paris by Anna), army shoes on my feet, and Dave wore a brown leather jacket and the biggest pair of huaraches ever *hecho en Mejico*. On my head (complete sartorial splendor) was a white sailor hat turned down all round like a bowl and on Dave's, a mammoth wheel of a straw sombrero. Dave carried a machete, a gift for his brother-in-law in Wichita, and we took turns carrying a gallon jug, wicker-covered, of Bacardi. Our path was always cleared by a dusty gaggle of children, dancing, pointing their fingers, and laughing up at us.

But it's of Helen I sing. (The bastard is flipping his orange-colored wig again) Helen . . . grey-eyed and red-mouthed and tall as a tree, sunburned and freckled and laughing till she cried. Holding her soft little belly in both her hands and me holding her wide white hips, the only place the sun had missed, in my hands. The hammock, the bed, the cool floor, in the shade and in the sun, drunk and sober and just a little drunk, well and unwell (seize the moment) and standing in the chest-deep water one night at Caleta. Laughing. With Helen holding our swimming suits in one hand so they wouldn't float away.

Pay attention, you weak-kneed Puritan bastards, who either gave it up long ago or who never took it up at all, don't close your eyes and ears to this singing, sweating, salt-sprayed, flower-scented idyll by the crazy sea. Don't miss it. There's life in it. There's life in it still. She's dead and I'm twisted and gnarled now but there's life there. The water at Caleta is changed for our having stood there. The rain and wind and alien bare feet walking can't fill our sand hollows. Not ever. The walls at La Quebrada still hold her voice, her laugh, her whispers, her pain, her nutty, happy singing, teasing voice. The dance floor at Las Hamacas still feels, I know, her quick, brown, sandalled feet ("God, I'm drunk, Jimbo.") The hotel mirrors can't reflect as truly since her brown and white body, pink-nippled, black-tufted, danced and luxuriated and stretched and posed with mine there.

Don't scratch your crusted, balding, cold-eyed heads when you look at me. Don't take senile, constipated refuge in words like fantasy and hallucination. I know the notes and all the lyrics. I wrote them and sang them and heard them. The siren wail at three in the morning doesn't die out ever. It keeps moaning and wailing in new ears always and it stays, piercing and alive, in the ears that heard it start.

Are you swept along, my friend? Did I make you believe? I suppose not. Perhaps I didn't make myself believe, either. If I didn't, I'm sorry, Helen. I'm sorry and sorry and sorry. But whether I believe or not, I remember.

CHAPTER FOUR

Dave and I were sitting there in our fine brown-leather seats (maybe it was a second-class bus) as we smoked and screeched into Cuernavaca. Everybody squirmed off and started buying those short, fat, sun-ripe, pale-yellow bananas from hawkers and cart pushers and donkey-back vendors. And buying Chiclets. And crowding to the shady drinkstand by the bus depot door to buy cool, sweating bottles of Orange Crush and washing down the warm banana meat with foaming, orange-dyed gulps. Laughing and nudging and mopping at children's chins and bib-fronts. And a couple of steamed-up pachucos, deciding to squirt a little orange fizz on each other and giggling and hopping around in and out of the shade with their downy thirteen-year-old mustaches softly shadowing the ledge above their brown lips and shockingly bright teeth and shouting, "Olé," and scattering the crowd in little jumps and squeals.

Dave and I chewed and chomped a quarter-stalk of bananas; he had a couple of orange drinks and I had one. One of the pachucos ran into him and Dave gave him a little broken-field nudge with his hip and the Mexican kid ricocheted off at a ferocious, good-natured clip and, bouncing off the wall by the pop stand, turned back to Dave, making horns and ears with his forefingers and thumbs sticking up and out from his blue-black hair, made a big bellow like a fighting bull and pawed his bare brown foot in the dust. Everybody laughed, Dave especially, and he went over and bought the kid another orange drink.

I noticed the two American girls move away from the ticket counter in the dark, cool-looking station and stand, still out of the sun, in the doorway. I didn't stare at them because they were not, after all, spectacular beauties (Remember, too, that I was making a laudable effort to be true to Dolly Corso at this time. Otherwise, I would have been stretched out several nights before in the flower-bed of an ill-lit park in Mexico City with a rangy, aggressive college lass from Florida whose apparent mission in Mexico was to lose her girlhood at the earliest opportunity. I was also dissuaded by other factors. The park was public. I was wearing Dave's best pair of pants, and I didn't feel it was the sporting thing to bring them home grass-stained and/or virgin-stained. Also, getting down to foundations, this girl, intelligent and semi-attractive though she undoubtedly was, had an adenoidal, unhinged fervor which, combined with a pair of large, very soft, but virtually nipple-less breasts, not my favourite kind, left me less than uncontrollably horny) but they were – after all, Americans, and we were, for Christ's sake, in Cuernavaca.

We got on the bus first and sat down in our reserved seats and then the two American girls got on. I gave Dave a nudge and he glanced up and said, "Uh-huh," and went back to his Latin-American edition of *Time* magazine. The girls walked to the back of the bus and found seats there.

After the bus started up and rolled out of town on the road to Taxco, I sneaked a look at them. One girl had dark hair and a sun-burned face with zinc ointment on her nose and lips and she wore green sunglasses and a floppy straw hat. The other one was smaller with reddish hair. Pretty. She gave me an electric look just as I turned my eyes to the front again.

"Since I'm a redhead," I said to Dave, "I get the one with red hair."

"Let's flip for her," Dave said, reading on.

"You didn't even look at her."

"Don't have to, Jimbo. If you want her, the other one must be a dog."

"Why don't you at least turn around and look?"

"Let's flip," he said.

So we flipped. *I* flipped *my* coin. And I lost.

"You win," I said. "Good luck."

"Thanks." Still reading. "Good luck with the dog."

Right there I lost interest in the whole campaign. Good sport that I am, I pouted and stared out the window. And after awhile I went to sleep. When I woke up Dave was nudging me. "Wake up, sleepin' Jesus. We're getting into Taxco in five minutes."

"What time is it?" I said.

"About twelve-thirty. I'm starving."

"Will we have time to eat in Taxco?"

"Two-hour stop," Dave said, "and we got a lunch date. Mine is a pretty redhead and yours is – well, she's a girl, I think."

Dave had gone back to talk to the girls while I was asleep. Doesn't sound like Dave, does it? Smart guy, good-looking enough to get by, easy talker, sense of humor, lots of confidence. But when it came to making it with girls, he couldn't pee a drop. I mean he could if they'd let him but damn seldom would they let him. This day, however, he was apparently like the tiger who went to sleep a coward and woke up a killer.

Lunchtime. A shady veranda overlooking the pink roofs

99

of Taxco. "My name's Marj," the redhead said, "and this is Helen." Helen still had on the hat and the sunglasses and the zinc ointment and a sad-assed expression. She was sneezing and her nose was running. She was not only sunburned and grim, she had a cold. She was also wearing a wedding ring.

"You married?" I asked.

"Huh?" she said. Sniffle, sniff, sneeze, blow.

"I say it looks like you're married."

"Uh-huh." Sneeze, blow. Even through her clogged nose I understood she meant yes.

Dave was sitting there drinking Mexican beer and grinning like a Chinese cat and making dull jokes and quoting various Senators from his *Time* magazine. I, trying not to look at my sunburned and married bundle of germs, drank three beers one after the other. Finally I bolted to the W.C. and urinated nonstop for eight or nine minutes. Then I just stood around in there for a while because I had no burning desire to rejoin the spook.

When I did get back to the table, I started eating some Mexican mess (ordered by Dave), praying as I forked it in that there wouldn't be a recurrence of my Monterrey attack or my Mexico City agony. Dave, gorging and guzzling, eater of native dishes, drinker of all waters from all wells and puddles, scoffer at black-widow bites and blood-poisoning streaks to the armpit, said "Marj and Helen are staying here in Taxco." I thought, "Thank God," and I said, "That's too bad."

"But we'll be in Acapulco day after tomorrow." Marj smiled at me and I thought maybe it's not a lost cause yet. I smiled back and said that's nice, looking down at my clean plate and trying to decide what it was I had just eaten and whether it had been completely dead.

"And," Dave said, still gorging, still playing at foreign-affairs savant, investment counselor, and smiling seducer of loose redheads, "just to make sure they look us up, the girls are going to pay for this lunch. We'll return the courtesy when we see them in Acapulco."

Marj giggled and reached for her purse and said what a funny but good idea. Helen sat there looking defeated and dumbstruck.

Dissolve to Acapulco. The story's over or nearly over because you know now how it started and how it ended and I gave you a good idea of what it was in the middle part. There are only a few close-ups and vignettes and curlicues and montage pieces to insert.

You know already, or you guessed, that the sweet and smiling, silk-shirted-with-no-brassiere Helen who found me in Acapulco was another creature altogether from the zinc-oxided, sunburned sour apple who had shared our luncheon table in Taxco. Such a different creature as to be almost unrecognizable. The eyes danced, the lips shone, the teeth gleamed, the mouth sang, and sweet God in heaven, how she laughed.

Dave sat stunned by the radiance, stealing dreary side-long glances at Marj, his erst-while strumpet, Atlantic City winner, and answer to all men's needs. She sat now, bravely fizzling like the last seconds of a July Fourth sparkler, glancing uneasily from Helen to Dave to me and then back to her plate.

They were having lunch with us their first day in Acapulco. That afternoon, they left their own dreary quarters, never slept in, downtown by the harbor, and moved into our hotel, not for illicit reasons but because it was a lovely and inexpensive place to be.

How depressed they were, Dave and Marj. Helen and I were so obviously and gloriously jigsawed to each other's pattern that any other liaison between male and female seemed in those genesis moments, tasteless, heretical, and doomed to teeth-grinding boredom. And that's how it turned out for them. They feigned interest in each other the first day, masked ennui the second, and flew the scarlet flag of antipathy from the third day on. Dave, resigned to playing a passive role in relation to Helen (I would have fought him, bare-knuckled, for her), spoke Horatio to my Hamlet for the rest of our Mexican weeks. He spent his days with us (with Marj, sometimes, a logy fourth. She finally gave up the whole works, including Helen's friendship, and went back to Mexico City alone) and his nights, barefoot and profligate, God knows where.

Advocate of reason that I am or profess to be, proponent of know-thyself, know-thy-brother, know-thy-lover, I admit that I knew Helen hardly at all. I don't know what she thought, whom she admired, what she read, *if* she read. I never knew her husband's first name; I don't know if she adored him, endured him, or hated him. There was no talk of why didn't we meet yesterday or how will we face tomorrow. It was all adolescent, immature, let's eat up today, tomorrow there'll be another today. And when all the todays run out, then we'll chew on what's left of yesterday. Helen and me in the shower in the late, soft afternoon ("Hold onto the chain, baby, or the water don't come out nohow") not in passion, but just there, nuzzling and sudsing and rinsing, and laughing.

The first night, after midnight, we were in a cloistered crows-nest patio at the top of the hotel, a hammock, a folding cot, and one wall open overlooking the bay. We were lying on the cot and I said, the adolescent, thin-skinned romantic beginning to hurt already and eager to hide it behind some shield, "Do you do this often?" "Do *what* often?" she said. "You know what I mean," I said,

102

"fool around with other guys besides your husband." She lay there silent for a while. Finally she repeated, "Do I do this *often*?" I said yes, and she said, "Every week or so."

Because I am the kind of fool that I am and because at that age my particular kind of folly was of purer essence than it is now, I stiffened out on the cot like a dead animal. She lay beside me quietly and let me petrify. Then at last she reached over, patted me on the stomach, and said, "Baby, when you ask a silly question, you've got to be ready to take a silly answer." She stood up then and I thought she was going downstairs. I started to say something but she held my head against her so I couldn't talk and said, "Anyone for the hammock?"

Can you see this girl? Can you smell her? Probably not. But the fault if you can't is mine. She was a girl you would have very much appreciated. Or felt at one with. Or felt male with. Scholar that I am, I find myself, all the time, when reaching for high praise for a woman I love, or cherish, or admire, saying "She's a nice girl." I used to say that about Helen. I also used to say it about Linda. I still say it. Linda is a nice girl. Eva Braun is a nice girl. Ma Barker is a nice girl, etcetera.

"Screw the world. All but six. Save them for pall-bearers." Is that an epitaph? I think not. Not for me. I am a lover of the world. I have no desire to screw it or its citizens. Except for carefully selected, bright-mouthed, heavy-eyed candidates.

CHAPTER FIVE

I borrowed forty dollars from Helen and I never paid her back. Should I feel guilt-ridden? I don't. I needed the money. Without it, I might still be in Mexico, guzzling Orange Crush for nourishment and seeking out lady tourists with my hat in my hand. I used the money to buy a bus ticket to someplace in Texas. I hitchhiked home from there, stopping in Evansville for a three-night reunion with Dolly Corso in the back seat of her old man's blue Packard (interrupted one night by a state trooper who, catching us unmistakably bare-assed, had the poor taste to light us with his flashlight while we uncoupled and adjusted our BVD's and the stupidity to say, in an almost fatherly tone, "What do you think you're doing in there?") and before that for two days in Wichita with Dave's sister and brother-in-law where we were specifically instructed to keep hands off the Japanese maid. Dave, I learned later, ignored this request and in a series of lightning moves, trapped the yellow-skinned bon bon in the laundry room hard against the mangle where, without Oriental proprieties, he, these are his own crude words, "put the blocks to her." After a visit to the doctor and a chat with his brother-in-law, he learned that the order to desist had not been for the maid's protection, but for ours. Christian Science and penicillin prevailed, however, and Dave was able, soon, to pass water without pain.

While in Wichita I took a Pi Phi from school, Sally Easter, to a matinée performance of a gray and grainy Italian film. A small part of Helen's forty dollars enabled me to make this gesture. In retrospect this gives me a small conscience twinge. But what the hell, it was only a movie.

I should have sent her the money, I guess, when I got to Chicago but I didn't have it to spare and by the time I did have it to spare (this was the year I worked for that department store in Chicago, thus postponing my graduation and my theoretical marriage to Dolly Corso) I had heard from Dave that she was dead.

Helen baby, I may have eased you out of forty dollars but I gave you all the love I had in those weeks. I guess you know that and I'm sure it's more important to you than the money. In case I'm wrong, I'll give you the forty next time I see you.

Bring up the music, Sid. The fiddles and cellos, the bassoons and oboes and clarinets and the heartbreaking French horns. With the trumpets and trombones crying and the harp arpeggios by the bleached-blonde lady in the white organdy gown. Bring up the volume and the colored lights and play that corny, ball-breaking, going-to-heaven-on-a-mule music.

What I mean is I loved her, man. And none of my horse-shit jokes can sweep it away. I was a careless and cruel, cunt-happy kid but I loved her.

CHAPTER SIX

Linda (I don't want to be unkind or say cruel things
about her or hurt her but I can't help feeling she's a
wraith. One day a stiff little breeze is going to catch
her out in the street and pouf, she'll be gone) is being
very nice to me. She is apparently embarking on a
be-very-nice-to-him campaign. "I'm very nice to him
and he's very nice to me. We see each other all the
time because of the children, and it's all really quite nice."
She is exceedingly warm and pleasant to me. Little things.
Today she stood in my kitchen eating cold sausage out of
my icebox. She smoked five or six cigarettes indicating
her contentment, her reluctance to leave. She chatted
endlessly (a tireless talker she, the uncrowned queen of
inaccurate information) about the new car that she and
new husband are planning to buy. Meanwhile I sit, scratch
my head and consider my scrambling efforts to send her
a check every Friday. Definition of alimony: The fucking
you get for the fucking you got. Dirty but funny. Also true.
I am not, however, paying alimony. Only child support.
But whatever the words, the illustration doesn't change.
A dangling man, poor provider at best, scrambling to
support two households. I support myself in a manner
which is creeping closer to malnutrition each week.

But, what the hell, I'm young (eighty-two), healthy (I
was able to make it all the way to the bathroom by

myself yesterday), in good spirits (I clipped out all the ads for funeral parlors in Sunday's *New York Times*), and confident about the future (I patronize no dry cleaner whose service takes more than three hours and more often I walk sixteen blocks to Seventy-first Street and Second Avenue for the one-hour service available there).

But Linda *is* truly being remarkably nice to me. "Would you like new husband to bring the children to you Saturday morning? Would you like to keep them all day?" "Are you doing any drawings lately? You should draw more, you know." *I* know that but how the hell does *she*? "Have you found a place to live yet? Don't worry. I'm sure you'll find what you want." Sweetness, dimples, and honey in the horn. Why? Is it possible that after quite a few years of being liked, loved, hated, despised, admired, and envied on three continents in two hemispheres, I am at last being pitied? Does she have the gall to feel sorry for *me*? Does she at last, God help her, feel equal to me? Or could it be that she truly loves me now that she's not saddled with me or I with her? Does she lust for me, perhaps? Does the memory of our extended horizontal ballets still lurk under her peroxide crown? I think not. I would bet many, many Yankee dollars not. Does that surprise you? Did you suppose that I think of myself as a great or treasured lover? Never. I am only a dedicated one.

If I don't want the niceness and the sweet, genial, let's-all-sit-down-and-chat-a-while smilingness, what do I want? More important, what does she want? Ah-ha. I wonder. Let's try for this size.

"Linda baby, come back to your red-haired daddy. I know I was a bad boy but I'll be good now. We'll buy a forty-room mansion on Long Island. We can build on later. We'll have new husband's red convertible and we can pick out two or three more cars. And we can have new husband around too if you like. He can have my side of the bed. I'll sleep in the hall.

"We'll have marinated artichoke hearts, I know you love them, for every meal and you'll never have to wear a dress more than once. We'll never eat at home unless the snow is too high to get the cars out of the garage.

"We'll have an I. Miller salon in one wing of the house and a Bergdorf-Goodman helicopter will make morning and afternoon stops on the roof, carrying a squad of stylists who will pick up, deliver, alter, or just sit and flip through Harper's Bazaar with you in case you want to chat.

"The children will have a nurse each, a nanny each, a tutor each, and they'll be trained to say, 'Oooh, look at lovely mommy!' every time you sweep into the nursery on the way to one of your hobby areas. They will speak French fluently, ski and swim and dive and play polo and do all the latest dance steps.

"We'll have a resident tailor for their clothes (how's new husband with a needle, incidentally?), a riding master, a boxing coach, a swimming instructor, and perhaps we should have a pediatrician living in as long as Arthur has that cough. He'll probably shake it when he's at Oxford.

"We'll have musicales, a little Johann Strauss and Ravel perhaps, those intricate, difficult works you enjoy so much. And there will be a gallery where you can hang all my paintings which you now own. Naturally, I'll sign a waiver of community property so that if you should decide, again, that I'm too much for you, there won't be any question as to who owns my paintings.

"What else? How about a boat? A Chris-craft cruiser on Lake Mead. We'd better have a house out there, too. And maybe a small schooner at Hyannis. We can lease a place there from May (March, you say?) to October (December?). Very good. March to December. Then,

of course, there'll be skiing. I'm sure you'll be fond
of that once you try it. We'll need a lodge at Aspen.
Nassau, too. And Jamaica or Acapulco several times in
the winter. I hope you won't be bored. Palm Springs, you
say? Why not. I don't see why we shouldn't have a small
. . . (large?) a *very* large place in Palm Springs. Even if
we're only there a couple days each year, who wants to
pig it at the Racquet Club?

"I saw something today that I think you'll like. A
lizard-skin attaché case, just for credit cards and
charge plates. No, of course, you won't have to lug it
yourself. You can keep it in our town house on Sixty-third
Street. Whenever you want it, just signal on your wrist
radio and a man will bring it to you. You say it's a nuisance
signaling like that? Well, we'll work out something.

"Now – I saved the best for the last. I promise you we'll
travel. I know you're dying to do that. We'll start with
Europe. France first. Six weeks or two months there the
first time. Mostly in Paris. We'll do the other regions later.
Then two or three months in England, London primarily,
with lots of side trips to the countryside. Then good slow
looks at Ireland and Scotland. They're so often neglected.
I don't think we should touch Scandinavia until we have
several months we can set aside for it. Denmark, Norway,
Sweden (No, of course I won't see *her!*) Just a week or so
in Finland perhaps. It's damp and I don't want my sweet
baby to get a cold.

"Spring in Italy? Of course. Autumn in Germany *is*
beautiful. That's right. No less than a month in Vienna.
Christmas and New Year's with all the children along (you
can have a dozen if you like, dear, and perhaps we'll adopt
a few of other nationalities. Yes, I know the movie stars
do that) and all your odd relatives. Plus new husband, of
course.

"We mustn't overlook Switzerland and Spain. A month in Switzerland and three months in Spain. That's right. Ava Gardner *lived* there. Then perhaps it's back to New York for a little breather.

"After New York, a world cruise, perhaps. South Africa, South America, Mexico, Central America, Australia, Hawaii, India, Japan. We won't miss a thing. Then – home at last – we can sit down with our maps and do some pinpointing, pick out the spots we really want to take a good look at.

"How does all that sound, Linda? I see. All right, you talk it over with new husband and let me know what you decide. That's right, *I* pay for everything. Of course. You ring me. No, I won't be here next week. Luther's coming back. I'll be at the Salvation Army refuge for indigents. That's right. You can reach me there."

As I say, Linda is being nice. Civilized, cooperative, and gentle. Shouldn't I be grateful? Of course I should. And I am. Although I know that she's merely repeating a performance (Linda is *not* an actress. She'd be the first to admit it. Mimics Chevalier with the lip, but beyond that – nothing) that Joan Crawford gave in Loew's Theatre in Newark ten or fifteen years ago.

So bless you, dear little Linda, for your sweetness, be it sterling, ersatz, or swiped from Joan Crawford. Keep it up for a year and I may smile at you.

I don't look at her at all now. Not if I can avoid it. When she is chirping or when I'm answering in monosyllables, I look at Gregg or Arthur and smile sweetly. Jesus.

CHAPTER SEVEN

I went to see the apartment that Karin called about. It's a dirty, cluttered hole in Greenwich Village, a place that no self-respecting human would voluntarily inhabit. But it's cheap. So I'll take it for two or three months.

The present tenant, my landlord, a bizarre type who collects parts of motors, old slot machines, broken bottles, and such, has promised to remove at least one layer of grime and to put the premises in some proper (I couldn't walk through the clutter from one wall to the other when I visited the other night) order. He asked me, with executive seriousness, if I ever sat down to write letters or anything. "If so, I'll try to find time to glue the chair together."

As I say, it's cheap and dirty and in a bad neighborhood so how can you beat it? At least it's liveable, I guess. But liveable or no, dirt, grease, cockroaches, dust, silicosis or no, I'm for it.

Having made this decision, knowing that I'll be roofed for a few weeks, I deposited my unemployment check, looking down my nose at the bank clerk who, snotty bastard, was very definitely looking down his nose at me, and came home to a spiced ham sandwich and a cup of coffee. Linda had finished my sausages (see above) in a ravenous moment while dropping off the boys.

At home, mayonnaising the bread, I was called by my New York agent who said she had received a letter from my new Hollywood agent (my old Hollywood agent, a wise and unique man of flawless character, died last August) suggesting that "interest was high" (an agent's phrase) and "activity hot" (another) and why didn't I get my unemployed ass out to the coast.

"I just contracted for an apartment," I said. When did you do that and for how long, my agent said. "Today and for three months." "All right," she said limply. "I'll write the coast and tell them that," leaving me with the feeling that I'd rejected solvency and immortality once and for all.

Here, friend, are the specific, crud-caked horns of my economic dilemma. Do I stay in New York, limping along from one obscure, underpaid show (there are a few, even of these) to the next, losing weight steadily as I count the pennies, lick the stamps, and mail the checks to Linda, all this so I can try to be a father still to Gregg and Arthur while they live under the wings of Linda and a man who is not their father? Or do I say to myself, "Don't deceive yourself, simpleton. Go where you must, work as you must, see your children when you can, as often as you can, but don't tie yourself to a floating buoy that will pull you, rootless and heartsick, into a stagnant backwater somewhere."

The decision is easy. In my circumstances, I have no choice but to go my own route. I thought I'd made the decision when I returned to California after the divorce. But I sold the furniture, gave up the apartment there, and flew back to New York like a predestined eagle.

The truth is simple. I can't leave the kids. You think that's inspiring? A tender, devoted father. Puts his children ahead of himself, ahead of business, art, everything. I think it's shit. It's weak and self-pitying and self-indulgent in the fullest sense. A nutty devotion that can be of

112

little value, eventually, to me or them. Nevertheless, I sit here almost contentedly tonight because tomorrow morning I'll get on the subway and go see them. A week from tomorrow I'll do the same thing. And a few times in between if I can. I'll surely sit here in New York in one sublet outhouse after another as long as my unemployment checks, my dwindling savings and my occasional residual checks hold out. After these end, I'll get an executive haircut, a few striped ties and a collar pin, and line up behind all those other miraculously liberated (from reality) shapes in striped ties and I'll say, "Well, now . . . all you friends and well-wishers of my squandered, piss-poor youth . . . the old boy gave it a try. And now he's going to sign up for a nine-to-five job with the rest of the crumbs. You think he's miserable? Never. He's only crying, Lawd, because he's so happy."

Since the robot stripe-tied people are well provided for, there'll be a fine, good-sized apartment for me, with a bedroom for Gregg and Arthur when they come on weekends. We'll have a lot of good, expensive times together, and laughs, and years later I'll hear one of them say to the other, "Dad's a sweet guy, but I guess he never had much guts." Try that for an epitaph.

A friend of mine, a handsome and successful child actor who, reaching his full growth, discovered he was five feet two and in need of a new profession (he now sells shoes) used to say, when he passed a crippled beggar in the Paris side streets, "No point in feeling sorry for him. He's gettin' his kicks."

Could I be feigning the harelip, the empty sleeve, the twisted foot, because I need to hear the moans from people passing by? Or is it my own moans that give me what I need? Neither. The Masoch strain don't fit my fiddle.

113

CHAPTER EIGHT

In the hopeless, drag-ass days of the Depression in our town in Missouri, an unbelievable thing happened. A local soybean processor announced that he would be building a new plant at the edge of town. Actually down in what we called the South End of town. Near the river and below the Missouri and Pacific tracks.

My father and a lot of men in town like him who had been out of work for a year or more since the zinc mill had closed, walked down and looked at the building site every day or so, always hoping to see bulldozers at work and a sign, perhaps, saying that laborers and hod carriers and carpenters were needed. Some of our neighbor men got out their tools and started sawing and hammering and doing repairs around their houses to get their hands hardened to work again.

When construction started, though, at the plant, all the workers were brought in by bus or old cars from Oklahoma. The local men were angry and a few of them wrote to the newspaper. Finally the paper printed a story saying there was nothing to be done. The contract was let to an Oklahoma contractor, he wanted to bring in his own help, and there was nothing anyone could do to stop him. The only local man they took on was a loudmouth nobody liked, a fellow who had clerked for two years in an A & P store in Kansas City. They hired him to carry water to the men.

The closest we ever got to the whole operation was through the Shaffers who moved into a flat across the alley from us. They'd come up from El Reno, Oklahoma, and Mr. Shaffer was the straw boss of all the laborers on the job. First my sister and I got friendly with the three Shaffer kids. Then their mother and ours started visiting back and forth, gossiping and snapping beans together. And finally Dad and Mr. Shaffer began smoking their pipes and drinking some home brew after supper.

Once when I was sitting with them on our upstairs porch, Dad asked about the grocery clerk and Mr. Shaffer said, "Ain't worth the powder and shot to blow him to hell." I laughed very loud when he said that and kicked my foot against the porch railing and Dad said, "Never mind, big ears."

One evening late in the summer, when the construction crew were working late, Dad and Mother and I and my sister and all the Shaffers walked down after supper to meet Mr. Shaffer at the job and ride home with him in one of the company's dump trucks.

It wasn't quite dusk when we got there and men were still working, pouring concrete up on the second level. We could see Mr. Shaffer walking back and forth on the edge of the forms, directing the men with wheelbarrows and the men with puddling sticks. He looked down and saw us and waved his hand. I was standing by my mother and I said, "Mr. Shaffer sure has a good job, doesn't he?" She squatted down beside me with her arm around my shoulders and said, "Honey, he makes a dollar an hour. Takes home a dollar bill for every hour he works."

Those words and the way she said them, like she'd looked out the window and seen an angel looking in, stuck in my throat and rang in my ears and ached in

115

my chest for days and weeks and years afterward. God, what that meant to her in those hopeless, sitting-at-home days. Can anything ever mean that much to me? Or to you? Or to her again? Never. Mr. Shaffer, high above our heads, waving and back-lighted by a blood-orange sun. And making a dollar every God-damned hour.

I have been paid twenty-five cents per hour on several occasions. I have worked for nothing but meals, for nothing but a room and a bed. I was paid four dollars a week for forty hours work. Ten cents an hour. I have been paid five thousand dollars a week or more many times and as high as two thousand dollars a day. I have worked up and down and in and around the wage scale, the salary scale, the commissions, share-of-profits, bonuses, residuals, and button-button, who's got-the-button?

Money means nothing to me because I have (literally) none. When I had a lot of money it meant something to Linda (she felt there was not enough) but nothing still to me. Numb. Does this numbness relate somehow to that sun-fired figure on the scaffold? Did I promise myself that someday I would equal Mr. Shaffer?

I don't know the answers to those filmy questions and furthermore, I don't give a good God-damn. Not about the answer or the question or Shaffer on the scaffold or a dollar an hour, or getting laid for a dollar or two hundred dollars or thirty beaver pelts, or swapping gum wrappers or matchbook covers (are you listening, Merlin Finger?) or movie stars' pictures or movie-stars' mistresses or any of the rest of the give-and-take, haul-and-shove, business-is-business horse-shit that makes the world go around so badly, miserably, unevenly, and incompletely for almost everybody except those who eat quarters, sweat dimes, defecate half dollars, and make love to old Brink's money bags.

Occasionally it occurs to me when my fifty-five dollar unemployment check arrives in the mail that it would be a jolly idea for me to send it on to my mother (now electronically stifled by washers, dryers, ranges, freezers, refrigerators, gas heaters, electric heaters, mixers, peelers, rotisseries, electric skillets, a covey of radios, a television with an Eiffel tower aerial, and other evidences of la dolce vita) with a short note attached saying – "See . . . I finally made it. I surpassed Mr. Shaffer."

Where are we? Are there loose ends? I hope so. The only neat well-ordered place is inside the bolted coffin.

CHAPTER NINE

Dave and I were coming out of Waco, Texas, on a hot July afternoon. Having just had a pineapple malted and two honey-cakes each, we had returned to our road-side position, elbows akimbo, arms aloft, thumbs pointing southward, when zoom-o, a red Pontiac convertible brakes down and slides to a halt in the road-edge gravel in front of us. A very acceptable (in her thirties perhaps) blonde is driving and beside her is her mother or somebody's (her husband's, later conversation disclosed) mother, not acceptable at all. "Jump in," said the driver.

As we hopped into the back seat, both Dave and I had a fast look at her white and luscious upper legs, bared by her perfectly decent and excusable desire to be, with her skirt lifted, less warm while driving. And she had a fast look at us looking.

"It's a hot day, boys," she said. She stepped on the accelerator, we jumped ahead, and she talked to us over the sound of the rushing air, turning the rearview mirror so we could see her and she could see us. It was going to be a short ride. She was driving only thirty miles down the highway before turning off east.

"But you might as well enjoy the scenery while we're riding, eh, boys?" She pointed off to the right then and said, "Look over there, Mother Nelson. Isn't that lovely?"

While sourpuss was looking away, Dixie (that was her name – Dixie Nelson) gave me a big wink in the rearview mirror, then reached up quickly and adjusted it so it angled down towards her lap. "How's *that* view?" she said. "Not bad," I said. She fiddled with the mirror again, moved her legs further apart and said, "Better now?" and I said, "Yes, it's beautiful now." "Yes, it is," said Mother Nelson, still staring out at the fields.

And it was. I said, "Slide over this way, Dave, and lean over. You can see the view on my side better."

So he moved over and we sat there staring at that marvelous Texas landscape all the rest of the ride. Lush and full and rolling. Real open country with nothing to block your view. And beautifully vegetated. Not blonde but beautifully vegetated just the same.

"Goodbye, fellas," Dixie said when we got out, "hope you enjoyed the lift. I'm sorry I can't drive you further."

We watched the car turn off and roll away and Dave said, "Drive you further, drive you further, drive you further," cackling like an idiot and hopping on one foot and winging rocks at telephone poles.

So goodbye, Dixie. Farewell, you sweet, fleeting moment in the Texas flatlands in July. Who's afraid of mother-in-laws? Who's afraid to spread a little innocent joy around the summer world? Not you, baby. Not you, brave Pontiac driver. Where are you now, sweetheart? In the junk heap with that juicy Pontiac? Are you over fifty? Damned right you are. But I don't care, Dixie, and I'll bet Dave wouldn't care. We're your friends. Lovers if you wish. Friends regardless. You befriended us – dusty, hot-eyed trudgers across the half-baked ass-end of creation. You took us in with a laugh and a flip of the hand, bathed our faces with the coolest possible air in the state that day and just for fun, just for the hell of it, just to be nice, you showed us that sweet thirty miles of highway like nobody had ever seen it before. Or since, Dixie? Or since? Be true, baby. Be true to the red-head, Dixie, and to my long, tall friend.

You probably think I exaggerate. Let me tell you something about me. I exaggerate in reverse. I diminish. I soft-pedal, mute, and diminuendo the whole fucking theme of the world. It doesn't need to be cranked up or amplified. It's there. All you honestly and joyfully have to do is open your eyes and ears and smell and taste and wrap it all up. It's very, very good if you'll let it be; it's very anxious to be very good. And how are you to know how it was if you don't spread-eagle those skinny white arms and receive a little?

For this sweet isolated moment I don't happen to be talking about women but even when I am, it's more than that.

A woman, to me or to any man who knows what he's about on this screwed-up, flattened-out (Columbus was wrong) earth, is not just a negative complement, a lover, a bed-musser, a bed-maker, a soup-heater, or any other one thing. To me a woman is how I feel about myself, what I represent, what I am. She's not all of it but she's a warm, responsible, integral part of it. A woman of any specific time, of any moment, represents me at that time, in that moment. If she didn't, I wouldn't be, wouldn't have been, with her, would I? She represents herself, too, and I represent her if she feels right about herself and about me. But she's permanent with herself just as I am with myself and no other single thing is so permanent in this or any other life; the permanent one-tenant occupancy of one spirit in one body – indivisible. One identity, one loyalty, one birth, one death.

Don't run from it, friends and neighbors. Don't take

refuge in the church, in God, in brotherly love, in family love, in children, in bourbon, cocaine, or self-deception. Enjoy them all if you like, if they're enjoyable to you, but don't imagine that there's a refuge there. Take refuge in yourself. It's all you got. (Right here is where the sermon gets hot). *Accept* is the key word, brothers and sisters! *Accept!* Now comes a voice (probably yours, cynical and atheistic) from the green-painted, shabby, and splintery bleacher seats where the skeptics sit (they don't want to be seen in the strong light at the front of the tent). "What about you, brother red-head?" (Is that a familiar neighborhood voice? No matter.) "What about you? Do you practise what you shout?"

No, heckler, that's why I preach so loud. It's difficult for me to accept anything. But I accept better now than I did before. I don't open my eyes and mouth nor my nose and ears to any scent or any song or any sky. Not fully. But I *want* to. I can't smell or see or taste or hear very well at all. But, Jesus, I can smell and see and taste and hear better than I could a few months ago. When I was in California in the fall shipping cartons and selling furniture and wondering who I might turn out to be now, there was nothing passing into me or out of me. No pore opened. No brain fold pulsed. But I'm better now. I'm much better. I'm convinced that I'm infinitely better now than I was then.

Enough of all that. Let's jettison it. Let's stuff it into an old grocery carton, pack it firmly with excelsior and crumpled newspapers and cotton batting, seal it with paper tape, wrap it and tie it with wire and strong rope and mail it, with no return address, to somewhere. Anywhere. I'm better.

Linda (often drunk) kept saying to me those last months, "You're too much for me. You're just too

121

God-damned much for me." I've been in and out of and around and through those words eight million times, but I can't find solid ground. What did she mean? What does such a statement mean to you? And to her? Anything? Is it the light in the bayou or simply an inability to articulate? The genius makes, they say, a bad bedfellow. So does the lunatic.

> Now I lay me down to sleep
> I pray the Lord my soul to keep
> If I should die before I wake
> I pray the Lord my soul to take.
> (If there's a better offer, I'll consider it.)

Goodnight, old friend. Goodnight, Gwen. Kiss the children for me, drain the cognac glasses and out with the cat. I'm going to bed.

CHAPTER TEN

Luther came back from France. I surrendered his apartment, cleaned, scrubbed, mopped, and polished by my own peasant hands, and taxi-cabbed myself, along with my nondescript luggage (including now a bag borrowed from Alicia which, even empty, is a backwrencher), my cartons, my fireproof file box, my oil paints, some early lithographs, and my one and only remaining painting, Phoenix from my autumn ashes, to my new cloister in the geometrical contradictions of Greenwich Village.

With detergent, sponges, and miracle cleansers and for thirty-six hours (time out to sleep) I scraped, dusted, vacuumed, swabbed, and rinsed. I crammed an already clogged storage closet with a broken chair, a kidney-shaped table, ashtrays, pipe-racks, faded prints of tiresome paintings by famous, untalented painters, and other maimed and stained bits of miscellany.

Am I a fanatic about cleanliness? No. I can live among the dust-bunnies and grit underfoot and webs in the ceiling corners and thumb-prints around the door-knobs and light switches as well and fully as the next fellow. I do like to think, however, that at least I'm *starting* clean or more important than that, in some order. The subsequent dirt, and disorder, then, will be mine and will give me the security of having sprouted from my own chaos rather than the day-in, day-out, year-in, year-out flakings and droppings of some other mammal.

It's warm in this place, thank God (cold as hell outside), and the water will steam or scald you to death whichever you choose. And the south window, painted shut for generations, can now be opened a distance of three fingers to let in the refreshing garbage air of the quartier. I've rearranged the furniture, losing a few crippled pieces (see above), and there's now room to walk, kneel, pirouette, or hoochy-coochy in the main room. I don't say living-room because although it *is* that, it is also the bedroom – what the foot-pad, cut-pocket realtors call a studio apartment.

One can pee in the bathroom now without fear that some virulent fungus will leap from the mossy bowl, scrubbed now to a blinding white, and fasten itself on one's pecker. One can prepare one's eggs in the kitchen without fear that the native air will putrefy them between tilting refrigerator and sputtering stove. And one can look at the tile floor of the entry way without puking.

Last night I slept for the first time in the bed (my nights are usually spent in the carpeted cocoon of Alicia's uptown apartment and in the brown arms of that tender lady herself) and woke up without bedbug bites, flea bites, rat bites, crab bites or crabs in person. So what the hell am I moaning about? I'm not. Things seem quite good here. Things, in reality, are actually quite marvelous here. I don't want you to sit in your tiled and landscaped patio, sipping a tropical drink, in a sun-drenched far-away land and moisten your cheeks over my living in this crummy Baghdad-on-the-gutter because, as I say, things really show promise of being genuinely outstanding here.

Anyway, here I am. The heart keeps pumping and the lungs sag and inflate; the bowels empty and fill and empty again, the nails grow and the hair. The skin

124

wears away and renews itself, the perspiration seeps, and the penis, schizophrenic supreme, bounces along, smug in a self-deception that the toilet function is its secondary one.

I am not at the peak of my powers, my energy, or my optimism. At such times I wonder how in hell I ever got to be the mélânge, mish-mosh, catch-all son of a bitch that I am. Full-time Christ, part-time evangelist, seer, servant, guiding light for the weak, the stumbling, the halt, the wise, the rich, the retarded, the destitute. Theoretician, healer, guardian of the art spirit. Who wants all that horse-manure on one shovel? Who needs it *alors*? I can't be all, or half, that I think I am, can I? And even if I could, it's too much. Too God-damned much. That's what Linda said. "Too much for me."

My brother-in-law says to my mother: "If you'd just stop being nervous, you wouldn't have those nervous headaches."

I don't like this line I'm on. I don't like the whole nutty connection. But I don't want to walk away from it or just stop or dry up or bog down. I would like to think through it, or talk through it or struggle through it somehow so I'll be able to swim in the surf again and ride horseback or fly in a jet. Just as though I had never drowned or been thrown at a jump or crashed against a mountain. You know what I mean so stick with me for a few thousand heartbeats. I'll find a way out.

Linda. Death. It's been a bad week in that country and they may abolish passports any day now. Or I may eat mine. Or light a large green cigar with it. Sick time.

CHAPTER ELEVEN

"Three months," Alicia said today. "Over three. Soon be four." It is all that time since we started. All that long time. And all the same time to the day since the divorce.

It's good with Alicia because she is a fine and warm woman and because, on top of that, she is making, with me, a specific effort to be fine and warm. This makes it not quite as good as it would be if she let it alone to be just what it is. But that is not, apparently, her way. Or at least it's not her way now – with me. She wouldn't understand at all if I said that I want her to keep her head on straight, her knees locked, and her eyes clear. "And some laughter in the tree-tops, baby!"

When I heard the month-counting speech it jarred me. The fine times with Scotch or martinis, the movies, the walking on Fifth Avenue in the snow would be squeezed out now in favor of the days-invested story, the where are we now, the where do we go from here? No more kissing through dinner-time and giggling and shall we go to bed or shall we wait five minutes? All that still of course, but different, with a new colored gelatin over the spotlight. Because the next act and any acts that follow must now, by dramatic definition, be played in a lower key. Not over yet. Not ended. But truly different.

So what do I do about her? Nothing. She is able to do all for herself. She has a blip on her screen at the moment and she can't quite classify it or shoot it down. It will go away, however, finally, and when it does, she'll cry for an hour, or a week perhaps, then she'll slide my photograph out of its gilded frame and that will be, in a large sense, that. Some incinerator attendant while picking his teeth will idly watch a grey profile curl and blacken in the flames and a glossy portrait of the new man (solid, prosperous, dependable, less elusive, less schizoid, less fucked-up) will find a shiny, like-new frame waiting on the bedside table.

Alicia will hang up her slacks and dainty apron then, fold her lovely, rough-knit sweaters in their clear plastic bags, slip her cook-book into its old resting place behind the spice jars, and examine carefully her sleek dresses and furs and slim black pumps. She'll have them cleaned and brushed and re-cut and re-fitted and polished and re-heeled with steel heels.

Then, one early evening, her hair freshly done in a new way (not pulled back over her ears as I liked it), her mouth red as an apple, her eyes outlined in black and shadowed with blue, she will cross her threshold, take the arm of this interesting metropolitan citizen (destined for my hole in the toothbrush holder, my towel rack, my half of the bed) and heels clicking, black eyes shining, teeth agleam, will descend in the wine-carpeted elevator, parade the wine-carpeted hallway, step crisply through the doorway and take her place once more in the shimmering world of theatres, night clubs, head-waiters, taxicabs, doormen, flash bulbs popping, and all the horse-shit rest of it.

Meanwhile what? *Je ne sais pas.*

Where is the red-maned lion who, at the drop of a petticoat, used to say, "You're a big girl and you're here because you want to be. You're able to take care

of yourself and I expect you to do it. I won't hurt you
ever. So if you hurt yourself or deceive yourself, don't
blame me for it."

Oh, life with the ladies – it once was so simple.

It once was so bright and so utterly fine . . .

CHAPTER TWELVE

It's morning now – my time of the bewildering day. Do you know what woke me? Melting snowflakes falling down my chimney and dripping on the powdery ashes in the fireplace by my bed. The fireplace is there, half the side of one wall, old umber bricks that have seen a few days and heard some breathing, and it burns hungrily. It's a delight and a warmth and a foundation. A really magnificent, scarred and beautiful floor-to-ceiling fireplace.

How can the days be other than bright and *plein de joie* and rewarding and rich and belly-warming and concentrated and full of the wonder of tomorrow and the glow of yesterday when I wake up in the morning, make a half-turn of my sleep-mashed canteloupe of a head and see, quiet and regal and infinitely solid and unbudgeable, the square, blocky, smoke-stained presence of this (how many years old – sixty, a hundred?) lovely old fireplace?

Enough. We divide up, don't we, all of us, into morning or night creatures? I plump for, yearn for, build my whole breathing and pulsing pattern round the morning. Noon is my dusk. My day slows then.

A martini at eight-thirty in the morning? I like it. Or at eleven. Or four. Or any other time until ten at night when I'm yawning like a child and ready to be put to bed. Garlic bread and lasagna with Chianti at nine in the morning? Not only acquiescent, I am eager. Liver and onions? Or zucchini? Pumpkin pie? Yum-yum. How about a frosty bottle of beer before your morning coffee? Pour it, baby.

Love in the morning? Of course. Awfully, awfully good and right and beneficial and all that. Does one get up and brush the teeth first and pass water and then come back to bed? I don't criticize that.

Does one have coffee first? Yes – if you like. Or if you both like. Or *no* if it doesn't work out or develop that way. Keep an open heart, *mes enfants*, and the world will reveal itself. Guzzle your tomato juice, gobble your eggs, your bacon, your coffee-cake, your toasted muffins, your fruit-cup, your oatmeal, your whatever. And have your evil, life-giving, black and poisonous coffee. Then, warm-lipped, full-bellied and pre-destined, return slowly to your smoothed-out bed. Dancing hand-in-hand, anyway you like it. Bedside music? All right. If you enjoy or need such bourgeois trappings. Lights on, lights off, shades open, shades closed? Any way, baby. Any way at all. Just drink in the morning, take a deep breath of the new day's air and do what destiny, and your pelvic thermostat require of you. The morning, the morning, la-la-la-la-la!

CHAPTER THIRTEEN

Rum is awfully good for you. Gin attacks the nervous system and will eventually be outlawed as absinthe was. Scotch is mother's milk. Bourbon destroys the brain tissue and will at last render you pink-cheeked, smiling, and utterly incoherent. Rye the same.

Aquavit will make you neither ill nor stimulated nor intoxicated. Cataleptic! A chronic condition if you persist in drinking it. Vodka is as dull and harmless as its parent potato, generally kind, however, to the human machine, potentially beneficial even, but interesting only when drunk straight from a wine-glass with dinner.

Tequila is very liable to open a new aperture somewhere in your body. If this is your need, your pleasure, or if you just don't give a damn, drink it.

Beer will turn you to flab, including your thinking-cap, and is the most dangerous long-term drink of all next to wine which as all France knows, will rot your guts, liver first.

You drink Scotch, don't you? You did when I saw you last, at the pre-wedding and post-wedding celebrations. But in college you drank bourbon. That's what we were drinking the night of that disorganized serenade of the women's residence halls when you sang a reedy first tenor to my baritone solo, falling then to your knees like a sledge-hammered steer and rubber-legging home later, supported by a bass and a second tenor, to be sick on your roommate's Thesaurus.

So is it Scotch or bourbon now for you? I suspect it's what's available. Or free. Right? That's all right. I, too, live off the land. I drink everything there is in bottles except bourbon and gin. Last week, however, when Alicia ordered vodka from the liquor store on Seventy-ninth Street and they sent gin by mistake, I drank that. Martinis. If you have to drink that juniper-berry, poisonous crap, drink martinis, and when you mix them, put a few drops of Scotch in the batch. Still tastes like gasoline but at least it's high-test.

The answer is: drink something. Beware of those glass-spined bastards who say, "Just a club soda," or "make it a tall one and very, very light." If a girl won't drink, that's something else again. She's either guarding her cherry or concealing the fact that with two or three drinks she becomes publicly what she has always been privately.

I knew a young woman, a health-food nut, who said to me, "You just drink because you like to get drunk." I said yes, dear, (at that time I was penniless and she was feeding me excellent meals as well as gorging me with her wheat-germ-nourished body every afternoon), but inside a little voice whispered, "No, idiot darling sweetheart. You are in error. I just get drunk because I like to drink."

Linda? Good drinker. Not as good as she thought she was and not half as good as she wanted to be and not as good after we were married and after the boys were born as she had been in the whirligig Scotch-on-the-rocks courtship days in New York or the Dubonnet-and-vodka days in Hollywood. But she enjoyed it at least. I've never seen her shudder when the first sip slid down her swan-like throat.

She's really a lovely-looking girl in a flat and empty

132

way. I mean there's a loveliness about her that could perhaps shatter a person, or a whole crowd of persons, if it weren't for that sliver of obsidian somewhere inside that cools the first effect and puts a mustard-gas mist over the whole loveliness-scape, broken glass on top of the wall.

God, I feel strong and positive and world-consuming on this cold, rainy and snowy son-of-a-bitch of a half-assed February morning. It's Valentine's Day, Lord, and all the little lovers and fat lovers, and old, tired lovers plus the non-lovers who are eager to join up or enlist or be drafted, are busy with their pens and their verses and their telephones and telegrams and candy-store salesmen, scribbling and whispering and wiring and gifting the banal, blooming message to somebody. And if there isn't a somebody, to *anybody*. I receive but I send not.

I do feel great, though. I talked with Luther on the telephone and he feels sleepy on the one hand and anxious on the other. I talked with Alicia and she feels good but wary because I feel good. "She's devoted to you," Luther said. What does that mean? Isn't that the way you feel toward a grandparent or the way a spaniel feels toward anyone? Alicia, even if she were a dog, would not, I am sure, be a spaniel and I am not her grandfather or anyone else's grandfather. Not yet. There is, however, in Missouri, a girl of eighteen, recently married, whose mama was attentive to me and warmly attended by me (ancient history). Mama maintained, her happily married condition notwithstanding, that I, a callow, lean, and well-muscled (at the time) chap of barely nineteen years, was the pop of her baby girl. Though this child (cross-eyed as an infant, fat and still cross-eyed in puberty, and short, blonde, and pretty, though bespectacled, as a young lady) bore no resemblance to me, it might be as her mother

133

said. So I may be a grandfather when I'm forty. Before that even.

Does this intrigue you? Change any of your daily attitudes? Of course not. Nor mine. Those willow trees by the river where Mama parked her car those summer nights are still standing. She is still phlegmatically attached to the same husband. And the daughter, whosever sperm she sprang from, is off and running on her own. And I feel very fine.

> I'll go see Alicia
> I'll go see Alicia
> I'll go see Alicia tonight
> She's so devo-o-o-ted!

A one-sentence letter from Hofer (Rapallo)

"I am now engaged in a great internal war, testing whether this part, that part, or any part of me will long endure."

CHAPTER FOURTEEN

My mother's sister was very sick in the hospital last year when I went home. The first afternoon I was in town I drove down to see her. She was sleeping, under sedation, when I went into her room. The nurse said I could wait there so I sat watching my aunt sleep, feeling sorry for her and thinking how nice she had been to me when I was a kid.

I waited for nearly an hour but she didn't wake up and finally the nurse came in and took her pulse and said I might as well go and come back later because she might not wake up now until dinner-time.

Just before I left the room I put my hand on my aunt's shoulder, closed my eyes and said under my breath, "You're going to be better. You're going to get better and recover. Starting now."

That night, when my folks came home from visiting her at the hospital, my father said, "She ate all her dinner tonight."

The next day she seemed stronger and the following day even stronger, and three days later Dr. Himber (who had hinted earlier that the situation was hopeless) told her she could go home at the end of the week. In a month she was strong and well again. And she's well today. No relapse.

Do you think I cured her? *I* do. I admit that I don't really *know* it, actually, but I strongly suspect that I did.

When I was moving from Westwood last fall, a young couple named Tibbs – Donald and Rose – answered my advertisement in the classified and bought the bassinet and baby scale and the crib that Gregg and Arthur had slept in as babies. When Donald Tibbs came to pick up the stuff, he asked me if I would come along to where they lived in Culver City and help him assemble the crib. When we got there, his wife was upset because their two-year-old boy was wheezing, trying very hard to get his breath.

"He has asthma. Always had it," she told me while her husband was calling the doctor. "We brought him out from our home in Niles, Michigan six months ago. Gene gave up his job and all. But the little thing don't seem any better here than he was back in Niles. He wheezes and gets so blue, I'm afraid some day he'll just choke from not being able to get his breath."

I walked over to the bed where the little boy was lying and while I was talking to Mrs. Tibbs and telling her that Arthur had had asthma attacks too for a while when we first took him to New York, I reached down and touched the boy on the chest with my finger-tips. "You're going to be all right now. You're going to stop wheezing and you'll be able to get your breath."

Tibbs came back from the telephone then and we put the crib together and just as I was leaving, the doctor came.

Last month I got a Christmas card from Rose Tibbs. It had been forwarded from my old Westwood address and had been following me around in New York for a few weeks. She had written a note inside saying that the little boy was much better now, that he hadn't had an asthma attack since the one when I was there. Did I cure him, too? I guess I did.

I told Linda one time that I would cure her headaches if she wanted me to and she said that if she wanted a witch doctor she'd go to Swahililand and get a real one (a pretty funny line for her). But she didn't go there. And X number of hundred dollars worth of Beverly Hills specialists didn't stop the headaches either. She should have tried me. She had nothing to lose.

I don't plan to hang out a shingle, you understand (I've never mentioned all this to anyone but you. And jokingly to Linda), or take ads in the medical papers. Nevertheless, I suspect that when the chips are down, when for one reason or another I care enough, I can do it. Don't take me lightly or I'll warlock you. Poof!

Once upon a time there was a warlock who fell in love with a lovely maiden. She loved him too, she said, and they were married, and the warlock was very happy. Soon, however, he began to feel sad because the maiden was so innocent and sweet and kind and he was, after all, just a run-of-the-mill warlock. So he tried very hard to please her and to give her nice things, hoping she wouldn't notice his shortcomings. But nothing worked. The harder he tried, the more un-warlock he became, the less contented she became. At last the desperate fellow, with a tremendous effort, purged himself of all his evil. Along with it of course, went his power to do magic. When the maiden saw what he had done, she left him. As he watched her walking away, he knew suddenly that she had become a witch and he was now a mortal.

What do you suppose the divorce rate is for warlocks? For those married in your town, it must be very high.

CHAPTER FIFTEEN

A postcard from Millard Hofer – a full-color photograph of the San Diego zoo on the front:

Who cares about the bomb? It can kill? So can gluttony. It can maim? So can a motor-scooter. El Bombo occupies no more space in my mind than the news of Sears-Roebuck expansion. Besides, it ain't really the bomb that everyone is twitching about. It's death, one of our beautiful guarantees. You get born and you die. Nothing else is assured. Do you want to avoid death and forfeit fifty per cent of your heritage? I don't. Answer by return mail.

Another card, postmarked the same day. This picture a portrait of two polar bears (brassieres added in red ink):

Why outer space? What about the orbit of the human heart? What about the intricate and lovely constellations of brain cells? The wonder of the hand, the miracle of the thumb, the explosive, tender beauty of coitus. Let's all feel pulses and swallow air and press mouths together and sing and laugh and examine ourselves like monkeys. Screw space!

These cards and the other excerpts from Hofer are all

from two years or more ago. Before the time when I answered his last four-page, single-spaced letter with a two-page blast saying in essence that he'd better get off his ass and off the booze and straighten himself out or he'd be dead in a year. "I'd help you if I could but I can't. And nobody else can help you unless you start to help yourself." I don't even want to hear from you again, I told him, until you can tell me you're doing something besides stumbling around every day in that God-damned zoo and slowly committing muscatel suicide.

I thought that letter might shake him up and make him take a clear look at himself. I assumed I'd get a crybaby wail by return mail listing his latest misfortunes. Not only was he broke now, having sold his last ten shares of Minnesota Mining to pay off an analyst, not only did his older sister refuse to talk or even correspond with him about turning over more of the dwindling, pissed-away-by-him, family funds, not only was his writing blocked for want of a typewriter, his clothes worn thin, pawned, or puked-on, but now, after all his drink-cadging, light-fingered friends had turned away, I, too, the only person he really believed in, the only permanent friend and confidant in his world, I, too, was casting him down, turning a stone ear and a hooded eye, suggesting he go back to Nashville, eat crow before his snotty sister and her husband (whose glasses Hofer had shattered with a lunging, drunken blow last time they had met) and ask them humbly to take him in and help him to dry out and get hold of himself again. Was that the advice of a friend? Did that represent the sympathy and understanding of a fellow artist?

But the anticipated letter didn't come. I thought, never mind – he's pouting. The letter will be here all right. Probably tomorrow. But it didn't come. It never came.

139

Linda and I talked about it and she said, Maybe you were too tough on him, and I said, somebody has to be tough on him or there'll be nothing left to get tough with.

I still think that was a very mean letter you wrote, Linda said. She had read the letter. She knew all about Hofer – as much as I knew. She had seen the snapshots taken in Switzerland and Austria and Italy and though she had never seen him in person, she had talked with him on the telephone. He had called the house long-distance from San Diego several times after he had seen me on television or when he was drunk and feeling sentimental about Europe.

After I saw him that time in San Diego and told Linda what a shock it was, we talked seriously over a period of a week or two about asking him to come live with us, the idea being that a home life with a baby around (Linda was pregnant then) and a country atmosphere and eucalyptus trees and regular meals and knowing there were at least two people in the world who gave a shit about him might straighten him out.

Linda was strongly in favor of our doing it and in fact insisted that it was something we must do. And I, who had suggested it originally and had laid out the core of the plan, decided at last against it. "He's really not the same guy at all now," I said. "I don't know who he is or what he's capable of. I wouldn't feel right about leaving you and the baby alone in the house with him." Linda thought that was foolish. She was surprised at me. He was my friend and he was in trouble. "Another thing," I said, "It wouldn't be something we could just walk away from if it didn't work out. He's looking for someone to hang on to and it would be cruel to let him hang on for awhile and then cut him loose."

140

"Whatever you say, dear. He's *your* friend," Linda said sweetly (this was in the first year of our marriage) but the lowered lashes and the soft shadows at the corner of her mouth said, "Shame on you, beloved husband. You're being disloyal and selfish. Shame!"

CHAPTER SIXTEEN

I had gone to San Diego to do some location shots. Sailor suit instead of cowboy boots for a change. We drove down from Los Angeles late one afternoon and checked into a hotel not far from the naval installation. As soon as I'd unpacked my toothbrush and razor I telephoned Hofer.

It was three years since I'd seen him. He had showed up in New York the week I moved into the Eighty-second Street apartment, only a few weeks after I'd met Linda.

He had been in Nashville getting his share of his father's estate put officially in his own name (before that, his sister had administered his share as well as her own), and he was light-hearted, hell-bent (a bottle of Old Grandad in his raincoat pocket and three more in his bag) and bound for Rome to do significant works. He looked great. Round and fat and pink-cheeked, a thirty-year-old man with a twelve-year-old face.

He stayed in my apartment for three days. I was running crazy at that time, posing for underwear ads in the morning, going to an acting class in the afternoon and spending the nights at Linda's on the Great Himalayan convertible sofa. I saw Hofer two or three hours each day before and after and inbetween my other stops. I hadn't unpacked yet. The furniture and paintings, packing boxes and crates were sitting where the movers had dumped them, here and there around the living-room.

Anytime I came into the apartment those three days and nights, he would be lying on the bare mattress, bottle and glass beside the bed, in his cotton sun-tans, socks, and a wrinkled white shirt, covered over with a blanket and the dirty tan trenchcoat he'd been wearing when I met him on a Norwegian freighter eight years before. Or he'd been sitting in a tiny area he'd cleared for himself at one end of the couch, wearing the trench coat (it was nearly zero those days he was there and there was no heat in the building pending the return or replacement of the furnace which had been dismantled and trucked away one morning by three fearless Puerto Ricans while the part-time superintendent was playing euchre in the basement of the building next door), hair slicked roughly back with water and a coarse-toothed comb; smiling, wheezing, coughing, chortling, and guzzling, the bottle in one set of pig-sausage fingers, a glass in the other, and listening, his head cocked to one side, finger metronoming, to whatever crystal Bartok or intricate Bach he could find on his portable radio.

"He's amazing," I told Linda then. "He looks chubby but he's hard as a rock. He hardly every sleeps. Seldom eats. He just sits and drinks and dreams. He says he went for a medical check-up in Nashville last week and he's in perfect health."

I had planned to go to the dock when his ship sailed but some work snagged me and I couldn't get there. So the image I held of him as we talked on the telephone in San Diego three years later was the red-faced, laughing Bacchus perched on the end of the couch in my apartment in New York.

"Can't you come out here?" he said on the phone. I told him I had a six-thirty make-up call the next morning. I had to get to sleep early. So I couldn't traipse to hell and gone out to his place, clear over by the back edge of the zoo. He didn't answer and I said hello, are you still there and he said yes. Then he asked what floor of the hotel I was on.

"Tenth floor. Room 1024. So hurry up."

"Wow," he said, "tenth floor. All right. I'll be over after a bit."

I ordered up a bottle of Scotch and some ice and made myself a drink. Then I started looking over the scenes we were shooting the next day. I learned my lines as well as they deserved to be learned, then poured myself another drink. I wanted to go eat but I was afraid Hofer would come while I was out so I had a couple of sandwiches sent up and ate them. I had a third drink then and the crazy bastard still wasn't there. I asked the operator to try his number again but this time there was no answer. As soon as I hung up the phone, it rang. "I'm down in the bar," he said. "Come down and we'll have a drinkee."

"Come up here," I said, "I've got a bottle." Big pause again.

"Yeah," he said, "all right. You don't want to come down here, huh?"

"No, for Christ's sake, come on up. It's getting late and I've got to get some sleep sometime tonight." He said all right and he hung up. I made him a dark brown drink and sat down to wait. When the ice in his drink was half melted, I finally heard a knock at the door. I opened it and said it sure as hell took you long enough.

I don't know if he saw the reaction in my face when I looked at him. I hope he didn't but he must have.

His head looked like somebody had put a tire pump in each ear and kept pumping until the skin and the flesh and the skull were just one tick short of the bursting point. The sweat was sliding down his face and staining his shirt collar

144

and making the hair on his head look slick and black –
plastering it in pointed, ratty sideburns against his cheeks,
pasty as unbaked bread. Christ, he was white. His mouth
was puffed up, lips liver-colored, and that great, inflated
head-pressure wouldn't let him smile much. Just a puffy,
meaty crack that looked painful and about to bleed as
he tried to push it into a shape that some pitiful child's
memory reminded him was a smile. His nose was a swollen,
shadowless roll and on either side of it, out of deep holes
in the bloat, two pale, irisless, pupilless, watery relics of
eyes peered, trying pitiably to show joy and friendship
but showing only havoc. Other than his mouth, the only
color in his face was in two deep-sunk crescents under his
eyes. Black.

You know me, my friend. I'm a tough, unsentimental
son-of-a-bitch. I've cut the testicles off hogs, seen foxes
beaten to death with clubs, disposed of a three-month foe-
tus in a subway trash can, watched steers being slaughtered
with a sledge, seen sheep get their throats cut, twitching
rabbits clubbed to death with a rifle butt, and I've picked
up arms and legs in a basket after a train wreck. I've got
a cold eye and a strong stomach. But when I opened that
door and saw the poor fucking corpse of Hofer, trying to
smile like a jungle brute still running after its guts are shot
out, I felt like I'd been hit in the back of the knees with
a club. I grabbed hold of his shoulders and put my arms
around him so I could look past him and not see that
soft-boiled face. His cheek was cold and wet as slime
against mine but it was better than looking at him.

". . . first time in over a year," he was saying.

I stepped around him and closed the door and we
walked back into the room. I said, what did you say,
and he said this was the first time in over a year he'd
been up above the ground floor of any building. That was

what had taken him so long; he didn't know if he could get up courage to do it.

"But I wanted to see you, had to see you," he said. "Haven't seen you since New York when you party-pooped and didn't come down to see me off. Big Christer and prohibitionist and party-poop and the devil's gonna claim you, sure as the world. Anyway, I figured for you, my old Europe drinkin' buddy, before you turned into a cowboy, for you I would by-God get in that elevator and come on up here. So I did. I did it."

He was trying very hard to be the old Hofer, the seven-or-eight-years-ago, even the three-years-ago, Hofer. He had the words right but oh sweet Jesus Christ the music was wrong and deadly enough to make me sick. I sat there in the chair with him on the edge of the bed and I laughed and slapped him on the knee a few times and said, "You son of a bitch," and "You good for nothing bastard" so he'd think I was right with him and didn't notice anything wrong. And every so often, I would push a drink at him. But I didn't look at him. I looked at his collarbone and his necktie and at the window shades behind him but I couldn't make myself look at those tiny swimming circles of wine-drowned eyes.

He was exhilarated, the poor dying soul, dancing like a hippo *en point*. He had triumphed over the elevator, the height, the bus ride (no wheeled vehicles for over a year either) and he was, in his own rotting blubber-mind, his old self, sitting in a kindred community, with a person who appreciated him, valued him, understood him, who would pander to his views, cluck over his misfortunes, commiserate, support and encourage. And listen. That above everything. Listen.

The speech, the articulation went last with him. It always had. He balanced on the bed like a pneumatic

146

Buddha and talked. Christ, how he talked. Crazy. It had always been crazy talk but shot through, sometimes, with gold. And a few tiny gold threads were still there. Behind the pus and waste and corruption, some pulsing miracle piece of that decaying brain still sucked blood and oxygen into itself, fed and cleansed its lobes and creases and wrinkles and sent still-glittering messages to the tongue and the larynx and the vocal chords. The Bach was gone. The full orchestration was burned out and sluiced away. But the solo instruments were still intermittently and spasmodically and heart-breakingly there.

Does all this tire you, my well-contained friend? Do you give a shit about Hofer? If you don't, then I haven't painted him accurately. And I haven't, of course. I can't. But he's not just another drunk. He's a gifted, brilliant idiot who had a lot to start with. But for some reason that nobody (he least of all) knows, he had to piss it away. I don't feel sorry for him but I sure as hell feel sorry. Waste curls me up like salt on a snail. It's the cruelest sin of all, the fundamental denial, the slow, drawn-out, painful, irreparable *no*.

"I knew when I saw you on the ship that first day that you were a good boozie. Course you always went to bed with the chickens. Never sat up in the card room and drank that fine Dutch gin, only twenty cents a shot. But you redeemed yourself in Vienna. Yessir, you were drinkin' pretty good there. And little old chubby Erica was hittin' that cold Austrian white wine and that drug-store rum like a real boozie . . ."

"Remember her in that bathtub in Zurich with all her clothes on and those big blue eyes about to pop right out of her head? Oh, I laughed like I thought I'd pee a quart or two right there on the hotel rug. God, that was funny. Me sitting there having a sippie and you in that God-damned

147

marble bathtub in the corner of the room with the curtain pulled around it. Erica was dressed up so pretty in her bright red suit and she gave me a wink and went over to the sink in the corner and got a big glass of cold water. Then she pulled a chair up next to the bathtub curtain and climbed up on it and sloshed that cold water right down on you. Oh, what a gaspin' and splutterin' there was! Oh, I thought I'd pee, I truly did. You stuck your head out of the curtain and said, "Once more and you go into the tub, clothes and all," and Erica sat down, laughing fit to choke, on the bed. But when you closed the curtain again, she just waited a minute or so, then she was right back up on that chair with some more cold water, winking at me again, and zowee, she let you have it. Ohhh, Lord, I was bustin' and so was she and you were splutterin' worse than ever. And then you came flying out of there, water splashin' and your dong a-swingin', and grabbed her, your hands all over soapy water, and plunked her down in that tub, red suit, high heels, silk socks and all, clear up to her chin in water. I thought I was gonna have an attack. She was sitting there laughing and crying with just her face stickin' up out of the suds and her mouth open like some kind of God-damned fish and I swear to Christ her eyes were as big as half-dollars. Oh, I never laughed like that before. *Never* laughed like that . . ."

He left at one in the morning, filled with scotch and high purpose. He would remember everything I had suggested because I was, after all, his best friend and I understood him, didn't I? First of all, he would tell that phony analyst to take a flying screw at the moon. Twenty-five bucks an hour and what good had he done him anyway? Told him he didn't really hate his dead father as he'd imagined all these years. Instead he hated his mother who died when he was twelve. Told him he didn't have a drinking problem. Had *another* problem, still to be pinpointed, and that's why he drank. "I may be a boozie, but I'm no drunk."

He would get rid of the analyst first thing. Then he would start writing again. "I'll sure as hell do that, get started on that right off the bat." He would finish a group of essays he'd started five years before in Basle and he'd hash over that old novel outline and see if something couldn't be done with it.

Also, he'd shop around for a part-time job, maybe in a grocery store, just a few hours a day to pay the bills until he was organized again and ready to decide whether he wanted to finish up his graduate work or look around for a college teaching job that would leave him with enough free time to do his writing. And most important, he would get rid of his friends, the ones who dropped in every afternoon looking for, or bringing, a gallon jug of muscatel.

"You won't be hearing from me for a few weeks, Jimbo, cause I'll be busy. But then, I'll shoot you a long letter with a carbon of what I've been writing. Think about that awhile. Maybe that'll get you outta those cowboy boots and back painting some pictures again when you see how good old boozie Hofer is doing. Yes sir. Well, goodnight and thanks. I knew I could depend on you. You're no party poop and you know what it's all about. All of it. Goodnight, buddy. And don't worry if you don't hear from me for a while."

"I'll hear from you when I hear from you," I said.

I heard from him the next night. I got home late from San Diego and Linda and I had a couple drinks and joked around a little and then we went to bed. We were sound asleep when the phone rang.

It was Hofer. I could hardly understand him. He seemed to be repeating what he'd said the night before, about his

149

plans, everything he was going to do. There was a lot of yelling and laughing behind him and then a crash like the phone had dropped off a table. I waited, listened to the party noises on the other end. He didn't come back on and finally I hung up.

The next morning at breakfast Linda and I started to talk about the possibility of his coming to live with us and a week or so later was when I decided it would never work. That day and for many days afterwards, she managed, very sweetly, to make me feel like a disloyal son of a bitch.

"It's me, Lord – let me in." Excellent epitaph.

CHAPTER SEVENTEEN

Do you suppose she always held Hofer against me? Did she sit on that divorce plane to Mexico and say to herself, "I should have known it would end this way. How could I ever be happy with a man who would turn away from a friend like that?"

All the time we lived there by the ocean with the kids and the cats and the horses stamping and running and snorting in the corral across the road, was that tiny brain clicking away like a vest-pocket computer, listing my faults, my transgressions, my limitations? Composing already perhaps, the eyes-downcast, small-voice speech to be delivered at last to some as yet unselected lawyer who would go home that evening and say to his wife that he really couldn't understand how some women could marry such worthless bastards.

"A lovely girl, not over twenty-five, was in my office today. Two children. She's heartbroken. Doesn't really want a divorce but she's afraid there's no choice. Her husband, he's an actor or a painter or some kind of bum like that, leaves her alone for weeks at a time while he runs off to California. To work, he says. Isn't that a hot one? And when he's here, he abuses her and turns her into a nervous wreck with his demands and his criticism. The poor child says, 'I do as best as I can,' and I believe her. I told her it would be a pleasure to represent her and hang that husband of hers up to dry."

If her lawyer, perchance, *did* say that, about hanging me up to dry, he spoke the truth, Horatio.

"All your friends are educated and smart alecky (Linda speaking) and they talk all the time about things I don't know anything about. How do you think that makes *me* feel? It makes me feel stupid, that's what. Nobody even listens to me when I say something. They just smile like they're saying to themselves, 'Isn't Linda sweet?' and then they go right on talking about some poet or some painter that I don't know anything about, that I never heard of before. I feel like an ornament. Nobody cares what *I* think, what *I* have to say. I tried to read all those books on the Impressionists, didn't I? And I read that biography of Gaughin and the one of Van Gogh. I make an effort. But your friends already know the things in those books. When I say something I read there, they just nod their heads and smile like I was a moron or something. They've all been to Europe a thousand times and they talk about it constantly. I've never been anywhere, except Atlantic City and Miami when I was twelve and this God-forsaken California. I'd *love* to go to Europe but I don't see anyone offering to take me. I'd like to go up on the Eiffel Tower and eat at Maxim's and see the clothes collections. I don't care whether *you* did those things in Paris or not and I don't *care* if they're corny! That's what *I'd* like to do. But I never will because you've already been there, you and your friends. You don't want to go anywhere. You just want to sit around and talk on the phone with your agent and read your fan mail and paint a picture two or three times a year. If you're such a big artist, why don't you paint more? Can you answer me that? You just want to *talk* about being a painter. Like all your smart-aleck, college-degree friends."

152

We're getting closer to the hub of it now. Name places, name names. What really *happened*? How did that cream-and-rose slender vision of an orange-juice poster girl turn into a hard-mouthed, vodka-eyed shrew? What fed her? What crippled and burned her and twisted the blooms off the bouquet? Who the hell knows? And who the hell should care or seek to know or find out at this late date, the air long ago having hissed out of the balloon? Who is masochist enough to want to struggle through tattered, other-day pages and faint echoes of long-ago words? Who is such a foothold-in-the-mud, nothing-to-be-gained fool? *Moi*.

Charades at a party and a woman (Linda's friend and mine), not cruel but careless, and speaking, after two brandies, her true feelings perhaps (Linda's theory), said, laughing, "Let Linda go first. *She'll never guess it*."

Heartbroken, little-girl tears in the car on the way home and a subject for painful words long after. "She practically called me stupid right in front of everyone." And a scar to carry for a long time until some new position of importance and being loved for oneself, of being thought charming and interesting, could cover it in proud new flesh. Could a few careless words, such a speck of flinty coral, have been the start of a reef of confusion and rebellion, growing steadily to an island of "Go to hell, genius. I don't need you anymore – you and your superior friends. And you *never* needed me. I was just a decoration, a decorative wife. You never loved me, not even at the beginning. When I got pregnant that first time, you were all ready to shop me off to Italy to have the baby. And when I got pregnant in Tijuana a year before we got married, you were the one who said, 'Take the shots, take the shots.' I didn't want to take the shots. I wanted to have the baby. I was scared

153

to death to take the shots. But I did it because you, on the long-distance phone from California, the big boss, said, 'Take the shots, baby.'

"And did you call me when I was lying here in New York in the hospital sick as a dog? Did you send a telegram or flowers or anything at all? Did you pay the hospital bill even? No. *I* paid it. The big genius was sunning himself beside the pool in Hollywood, thinking about God-knows-what, how you're going to change the world, probably. Well, you're not going to change anything. Don't you know that? But *I'm* going to change something. I've had your theories and your sweet talk and your stinginess and your big mouth for almost seven years now and that's enough for me. *I'm twenty-five years old!* I want to have some fun and enjoy myself. I want to feel important, too. I may not be as talented or intelligent as you, or have a big college education, but I have feelings and a heart and that's more than you can say. You've stifled everything in me. You're just too much for me – that's all. Too damned much."

Need I defend myself to you, my friend? Do the words, "Good God," come to your lips? If I were to hurl my rebuttal diatribe against Linda's, the one above, you'd undoubtedly say, "Good God" again. But why do it? Why dissect the cadaver?

Perhaps after all, there's nothing to discover. Perhaps it's simple and uninvolved –

> Old husband, new husband
> Cock-a-doodle-doo
> I think I'll find me
> Number Two!

What about that? Possible? Very possible. Rather than a complex mathematical sequence perhaps it was merely an old and simple equation: $1+1+1=3-1=2$.

CHAPTER EIGHTEEN

I sat in Striebel's office, the windows looking out past the Belmont Hotel toward the edge of the lake. I had just told Striebel, a gray-haired, vice-president grown lushy and arthritic during long years of moving sofas and twin beds off the dealers' floor by the power of his written words, that I was leaving in two weeks for Europe, chucking the whole ruddy works.

He looked at me, steel-rimmed and hard-eyed (he, not me. I was smiling and hangover-eyed), then he swiveled away and stared for a long time at the lake, fingertips pressed lightly together. I had seen this effect two hundred times at least. When he turned back there would be a new slogan for the dealer, a new approach to the jobber, a new point-of-sale message, a time-tested media recommendation.

He swiveled back now, raised one stout forefinger in the air and said in organ tones, "When you go back to your own office, I want you to look at the date on your desk calendar, memorize it, and never forget it. Because all your life you're going to say to yourself, '*That* was the day I made my big mistake.'"

"Why?" Striebel wanted to know, *Why* would I want to leave this womb of security and opportunity? I had no answer for him. But around the office there were many answers. "He's going to France to paint crazy pictures."

"He's probably got somebody knocked up." "He had a better offer from a company in the east – he's not going to Europe at all." "He's probably going to New York, to shack up with that Dort what's-her-name, that big brunette he was going around with last year." "He's a good guy. I'm glad he's getting out of this rat race." "Good riddance. He's a prick."

The real reason I was leaving – not the total reason, perhaps, but the trigger at least, was a tall, brown-haired Siamese cat-girl from Winnetka. Twenty-eight years old, four children and recently divorced from a Milwaukee department store fortune. I had tried to call her at the hospital two Sundays before my talk with Striebel (I'd been calling every hour for the three days since I'd heard about the sleeping pills and I'd never been able to reach her) and finally someone other than a nurse had come to the phone, her spindle-legged, henna-haired slut of an opportunistic, greedy mother. "Yes, Gloria did get your messages. She's much better, thank you. You mustn't be offended, but she told me to ask you please not to call again. Her fiancé's here now from Palm Springs and . . . well, you understand."

So I got drunk and got laid a few times by some friendly neighborhood stenographers and finally I called up a steamship line and said, "Get me out of here."

Later, after my moment of truth with Striebel (and a trauma with my parents who said optimistically, "You'll never get another job. The word will get around to all the business leaders that you're a quitter and you'll never get hired again. You're probably not quitting at all. They must have fired you.") I was sitting in the bar of the Palmolive Building one afternoon, three days before I was to leave for Europe, sipping scotch with a couple of friends, when Gloria swooped in with some bland eunuch and sat down directly across from me, chin in hand, her soul pouring out of her beautiful, slanted cat eyes for me and all onlookers to see. I got up and went to the toilet and when I came back, I sat in another chair with my back to her. After a while, a waiter came over with a note but I didn't take it from him. I said, "Tell her no." Hard to get? Not me. I was hurt, buddy. She'd worked me over pretty good. And I was eager for more if I let myself go. That's why I couldn't look at her or talk to her. I was afraid to.

When I got up and left the bar, she followed me out into the hall and said, "Please, I have to talk to you. Will you be at your place at seven?"

"I'll be at the airport. I'm leaving for New York at seven-thirty."

"Dort?"

"No. I'm going to France. I'm sailing Thursday."

"Why?" she said. "Why are you doing that?"

"I want to."

"But when will I see you?"

"You won't," I said.

"I love you so."

"Horse-shit."

I walked home, called the airport, and changed my reservation to the next morning. I sat in my room drinking for an hour or so and then I strolled over to a ceramics shop on Rush Street where the proprietor, a sloppy fat girl with a cast in her left eye had been giving me cock-eyed but meaningful glances for several months. She closed the door when I came in, pulled the shades, and led me into a back room. She took off her glasses and I took off her dress and I spent the night in a heaving, wallowing clutch that was as far from Gloria's smooth undulations as I was ever like to get.

When I came back from Europe four years later, I

dropped into the ceramics shop again. I didn't recognize the girl. She'd had her cock-eye operated on and she'd lost about fifty pounds. She was stunning and cologned and confident and quick as before to close the shop. She undressed proudly and slowly now in the full rose light; she strutted and pirouetted and smiled. Then she pulled me down on the cot and screwed me gracefully like the svelte, attractive lady she had become. And it was lousy.

CHAPTER NINETEEN

Gloria. I met her at the home of the same man who, two years earlier had introduced me to Dort. He and his wife were social, well known, newspaper-photoed, and very happily married. The men who slept with her and the women who spent long lunch hours with him in a suite at the Ambassador East were convinced always that these two superior creatures were well-met and well-mated.

At the time I met Dort there, I believed every varnished inch of their marital canvas. The wife slim and quick-witted (smartly, famously vulgar), all tight-curled and hostess-gowned and barefoot dancer late in the evening. And the mate, casual, long legged, and self-effacing, scotch decanter ever in his Princeton-ringed hand. And their eight-year-old twins, a boy and a girl, both with clever, unusual nicknames, running in in their night clothes for handshakes all round and goodnight hugs from the magnificent parents.

By the time I met Gloria, however, my eyes saw more, my wisdom was endless, my sensibilities dulled to the right and sharpened to the left. Heavy-lidded, red-lipped, beginning at twenty-five to be alcohol-paunchy, I knew, sneeringly and sensually, what was expected of me. Dort had been shuffled and dealt to me to break the rhythm of her bedship with the casual, long-legged husband. A successful tactic for all concerned. That phase completed as far as anyone knew (Dort had moved to New York that winter), I was now to be offered up to the latest friend of long-legs as a diversion, a consolation gift, an obliging orgasm gadget. I cared not which. I squatted like an erotic toad in those days, glass-in-hand, sleepy-eyed, tongue flicking out swiftly from time to time to take any bright flies that tarried too long in range.

To make a great omelette, grease skillet not with butter but with cooking oil. Big difference. Linda was frightened of making omelettes but she made an excellent mousse chocolat. Synthetic but delicious. And once, early in our courting days, she made a succulent, unbelievable sauce Bearnaise. Two nights in a row. But never after that.

I turned to Gloria from the beginning like a light-starved flower to the sun. I sniffed the corruption under the Arpège but it didn't matter to me. Not only did it not matter but I clawed and beaked at it like a carrion-hungry bird. Her hands, slender and brown, were always on me those weeks, their warm, homing touch as thumpingly familiar to me as my own heartbeat.

Her hair was straight and black and greasy; in the time I was with her it was never washed, seldom combed. She never took off her exquisite jewelry. She wore only black dresses, low-cut and expensive, usually spotted faintly from wine or food, opening often at one seam or another, or uneven at the bottom where a run-over spike heel had caught in the hem. She boasted that she never wore a brassiere or any other piece of underclothing. Cologne, a diamond necklace, diamond bracelets and rings, black dress, pumps, and a sable coat. Or on warmer days a hip-length sable jacket.

We were usually with her putrid friends on the north shore – the men puffy and milky-eyed and the women laughing and bending and dipping over in low-cut dresses

161

to show their tough brown nipples. Or on hands and knees with the dice on thick beige or white carpets. Champagne suppers and champagne breakfasts and cocktails all night. Or midnight barbecues. And the mushy smiles on every mush-faced bastard at every party announced that he had known or expected soon to know the brown hands and humid presence of sweet Gloria.

Who could be drawn to such a girl? *I* could. Any time, any terms. I had my nickel in my hand ready to take the long ride, no matter where.

She had no alimony. Ex-husband's revenge for her towering adultery record. What did I care? She was forty thousand dollars in debt. That's all right, baby. She had four children ranging in age from eight years to seven months. What did *that* matter? She had a blood-sucking, pimping mother who had already selected her daughter's next husband, a simpering alcoholic wreck from Palm Springs who had a foot fetish and uncounted millions from the cereal business.

"I hate him but what can I do?" sighed God's fallen sparrow. "Somebody has to pay my debts."

"Don't worry," I said, "things will work out for us. And I promise you, you're not going to marry that son of a bitch."

"All right," she said, "whatever you say. Maybe we'll load the kids in the car and take off for Canada. You and me and the kids and to hell with everybody."

"That's right," I said, "maybe we'll just go to Canada and drive around all summer and have fun and then we'll go down to New Orleans or Sarasota or someplace and I'll get a job and things will be fine."

The next day she tried to kill herself with sleeping pills. My friend at the office who had introduced me to her told me about it. That's when I started the string of phone calls that ended in the murderous conversation with her crap-hound mother.

But what the hell, it didn't kill me. It got me out of Chicago and it got me on that thirteen-day freighter and it got me to France, walking down the road to the center of myself. So that's not bad, is it? Just my birth day, that's all. So maybe I should look on beautiful, dirty-necked Gloria with greater charity. Maybe.

I heard from her about six months after I arrived in Paris. She had got my address from God-knows-who. She was living outside Dallas and she hadn't married the rich drunk after all. Most of her three-page letter was devoted, so help me, to a detailed genital description of a roan stallion that belonged to her neighbors across the road.

Seven years later, when Linda and I were living in Encino and Gregg was about five months old, I heard from her again. She had written to me in care of the network. She was living in Denver now and in a month or so, she planned to spend a week in Beverly Hills. Maybe we could get together for an afternoon. I think that's the way she put it. I found the letter in our mailbox one morning on my way to work; I tore it in little pieces while I waited for the light to change. As I drove down Laurel Canyon toward Sunset, I rolled down the window and sprinkled the pieces in the street a few at a time.

When I got home that evening, I was sitting on the couch giving Gregg his bottle and Linda was sitting with me having a martini. I thought about the letter and how worthless and aimless and long ago all that chaos with Gloria seemed and how fortunate I was to have waded through so much mud and crap and come out finally on dry and solid ground. With a lovely girl who cared for me and a fat healthy son.

CHAPTER TWENTY

Hofer on Art (Zurich)
I want to see and feel the jagged places, the stops and starts, the indecision, the mistakes, the erasures, the red area that was painted over with raw siena but still shows its redness, the paragraph that stops short of perfection. I want to see, not a gleaming, tasteful, unified, craftsmanlike product, but the stumbling tracks of an imperfect, sweating human in an unquiet battle with himself and his world.
Hofer on Life (In conversation in Paris)
The inner life is the only life.
Everything else is ballet.

When I think of that puffed face, that young brain slowly marinating, the tongue growing thick, the throat closing up, the fingers swelling and stiffening and rubbing together fatly . . . Jesus.

If I drink one cup of coffee in the evening after dinner, I lie awake like a round-eyed child for hours (a Danish sociologist said in 1900 that this would be a century of children. I am unquestionably born to it. You, I think, are of another century). Coffeed awake last night and staying here alone while Alicia kept some platonic, she insisted, rendezvous (she's impatient with me because I'm not jealous), I started thinking about Linda. Not in relation to me or to new husband or to Gregg or Arthur but to her own unlikely self. Perhaps it was the softness of the night or the warmth of my bed but for some reason my thoughts touched her more gently than they have at any time since we were cut apart at the brow like skull-joined twins.

Linda is a meatless meal, a Viennese creation of ice cream, meringue, and pale fruit with whipped cream heaped on top. She is what she pretends to abhor, a decoration. I say this without cruelty or bitterness. I would like her to be, because I know its value to her, the most treasured creature in sight, known and sung as such. Realizing she is not that and knowing she will be each year a bit further from that, I weep for her and the hollow, unfulfilled cut-out she could, God forbid, become.

"Save your concern, you fool. Dwell a moment on your own shortcomings. Besides, she may suddenly find herself and extend and expand admirably and incredibly. She may stand for Congress, she may write a volume on ethical contradictions, she may reappraise Schopenhauer or Pound." Or she may spend her days slobbering into the phone and leafing profoundly through fashion magazines. More likely, *mon vieux*. Much more likely, the latter.

CHAPTER TWENTY-ONE

When chaos exists, order is the answer, is it not? Make neat mounds of dirt, or hay-cocks, or firewood-cords. Stuff laundry bags, polish shoes, untie the knots in string, sharpen pencils, empty dust-bins, make patterns of paper clips, pay bills, write letters. Order. Select a morning newspaper, buy it each morning at the same time. Choose a market-day and a market. Go there and push a wire cart, rubber-tired, through the bright-labeled aisles, list in hand. List written on a three-by-five file card taken from a stack of such cards kept, and regularly replenished, at the top right-hand corner of the desk.

Detergent (eight cents off regular price), whole wheat bread, one dozen medium-size brown eggs in a blue-and-white pasteboard carton. A light bulb to replace the burned-out entry-way bulb, three one-pound packages of ground beef. Cookies with cream centers for Gregg and Arthur when they come to visit, and rolls of fruit mints for them. Two cans of peaches (Elberta) for their cottage cheese and fruit lunches. A week's supplies, at least. Two arm-breaking bagsful to tote from the supermarket on Christopher Street. Among the duffel coats and beards and berets and corduroys and Levi jackets and sneakers and desert boots, I, in my sleek black shoes, handsome plaid topcoat, cashmere muffler and carefully trimmed hair, look like an emissary from elsewhere. A federal investigator, perhaps, checking visitors' papers, a successful playwright flushing color for a new scene in the second act, a young public relations man, with a wife and a co-operative apartment in the East Sixties, grocery-shopping for his twice-a-week mistress who wears long black stockings and an Italian trench coat and lives in a studio overlooking Sheridan Square.

Order. It's coming, I think. Till it arrives, however, definitely and finally, I have to keep on making patterns, charting maps, following them. Redredging old gullies, cleaning drawers, emptying files and baskets, folding blankets, washing socks, listing seen places and known faces and things that sank in or stayed out. Lining it all up in rows like the sharpened pencils or the paper clips. Examining, discarding, fingering and handling and mulling over. Scratching through the dust and the dirt for fingernails and fingers or arms and legs, or genitals or tufts of hair or patches of skin that fell off or wore off or were pulled off or scraped off me. And trying, very deliberately, to find the place on my body where each scrap fits, or the shadowy niches inside my skull where the tiny pink-grey brain hunks belong. And the places (harder to find) inside the brain-hunks where the nervous, sweating bits of fear and memory and vengeance and sweetness and cruelty can be tucked and folded to sleep, to mend themselves in soft darkness until they're able to mesh again into the tough, beautiful pattern of whatever it was I was doing or being before last summer.

Order, I'm sure, will do it all. But, Christ, it's a bitter, wandering process. Picking up stones one by one in a field of gray and pastel gravel that stretches as far forward and back and to either side as my dried-out eyes can see. Turning the stones over and feeling each one, sniffing and tossing away finally and picking up another and not knowing or even pretending or hoping to know as I paw through the grit and the dirt what it is exactly that I hope or need to find in that broad pebbled field. But knowing nonetheless as I bend and straighten, toss away, and bend again that all the bending has to be done until – what?

Perhaps there's a stone somewhere here that is a different shape or a different color. If not, then I must conclude at last that a thousand futile searchings and pawings through the same unfruitful gravel are better than the dry-mouthed assumption that no search is possible or worthwhile, that no search can uncover the pebble that will somehow keystone a wall for me to stand on or hide behind. I can't assume that. I refuse to assume it.

Hofer (Paris)

If all I am is what I *feel*, then I'm a lost bastard because I feel hollowly and corrosively, unendingly bad. If I am, however, what I *think* I am, I will certainly glow, grow, and survive in green-leafed splendor. With deep roots and buds and stems and shoots and tendrils and leaves and thorns (why not), and velvety, blood-red, savage and frightening blossoms. Yeah!

When I lived in Paris, I kept a written record of things that happened. Regular, but not daily. An impersonal listing of facts, dates, events, and places seen. And once in a very great while, something intimate or personal. One night, after a good day of work, an excellent dinner Chez Wadja, a tender two hours with Erica in her goose-down bed at the Hotel des Etats-Unis (this was before she moved in with me), a slow stroll along Boulevard Montparnasse, and a midnight white wine at the Kosmos,

I sat in my seventh floor room and wrote, "Sometimes the world seems cut so specifically to my particular set of dimensions, the joy is frightening." I felt that way often in those days. And I'll feel that way again, I know. But not yet.

PART THREE

CHAPTER ONE

When I was painting every day, I used to get up in the morning and before washing or dressing, I would turn on the light or open the curtains and look closely at my work of the day before. After I became an actor, I discovered (the discovery, the realization, came some time after the habit had formed) that when I got out of bed I went to the mirror to look at *myself*. Vanity? I don't think so. The reflection did not please me. What I looked for in my face (I do not have that morning mirror habit any longer) I did not find there, have *never* found there. I see only a half-hidden meanness which must prompt my sister's frequent remark, "Everyone else is afraid of you, but I'm not." She *is*, however.

I avoid mirrors now except when shaving and I have speeded up that process so that I only have to look in the glass for a few seconds, often with the bathroom light off. Aside from gray reflections in shop windows, subway train windows, or in the mirror over Alicia's dressing table, I am able to avoid my physical self. It is four years at least since I have had the courage, the curiosity, or the stomach to watch myself on television or in a motion picture. When I see a still photo or a snapshot of myself, the face seems flat and alien to me.

And the inner man or inner boy or inner dog or inner whatever-is-in-there – can I look at him? Yes, more easily.

I made him. I could look at him better these last months, however, if I could locate him. I hear mumbles and moanings, even chuckles from time to time but he's elusive, out-of-sight, tempting me to reach in and drag him out wailing, breech birth or not. My hands are not ready, however, for such a delivery. Not yet.

I had sardines and toast for breakfast and an egg sandwich with *café au lait* for late three o'clock lunch. It's six o'clock now and dark outside already and the kids have stopped playing in the streets and I'm sitting, head-in-hand, eyes darting here and there from scotch tape spool to rubber cement can to white-paint jar to fountain-pen ink, to razor blades and paper clips in a pen-point box, to drafting tape and fixatif, to pencils in a cup and brushes in a beer mug, and I'm so God-damned hungry my eyes aren't focusing. I guess I ate too much yesterday.

It was Sunday. Casa Alicia we had roast beef Saturday night, voracious love Sunday morning. Then we read the paper, took a nap, and had eggs and coffeecake and coffee at three o'clock in the afternoon. We came home from a dreary double feature at nine o'clock, had a few glasses of rum (I, not the Señora), supped on potato salad, cold chicken, garlic bread, marinated herring, and beer.

I woke up at three-thirty in the lousy jack-ass morning, drank five glasses of cold water, ran cold water on my wrists, slopped cold water on my ankles, opened the window further, got back in bed and gazed at the ceiling until seven-thirty. I got up then, took a shower, got dressed, kissed the sleeper, set her alarm for nine-fifteen, and came home by subway.

I bought bread and detergent at the corner market, stopped for my clean shirts at the laundry, picked up a letter from my insurance agent (Linda is being displaced as my beneficiary), came upstairs, fiddled around a while, read the morning paper, and then ate my excellent toast and sardines.

I shouldn't be so hungry now. Often I have only two meals a day. But not today. It's because of the late meal last night. Stomach fed frequently demands to be fed frequently. Stomach fed seldom content to eat seldom. This wisdom was gleaned from a *clochard* under a bridge in Paris.

CHAPTER TWO

Luther tells me he saw Anna in Paris. She married after
I saw her last nine years ago. And divorced. And she has
a six-year-old son. She has given up sculpture now – she
was not a good sculptor so it's good she gave it up –
and is painting (on the easel I left with her, I'm sure)
and is selling enough of her work to support herself and
her child.

She has a studio near Alesia and she is still lovely,
Luther says, although a different woman from the days
when I knew her. I don't know exactly what he means by
that. In the four years I knew her, she remained lovely but
was somewhat less lovely at the end than she had been in
the beginning. Her lips had grown thicker, her skin less
radiant, her nose and her face had begun to coarsen. Her
ass, muscular and specific always, had begun to be, in
her tight boy's slacks, a caricature of itself. Her brilliant
eyes, outlined, shadowed, accented, had started in those
last months, to grow dull and surly.

"Why won't you ever talk to me about painting?"
she used to say at least once a day. Usually, after our
post-luncheon nap while she washed herself slowly and
carefully, like a soft brown cat, at the douche bowl. Also
each day at this time she made, before she left for work, a
cup of tea, heating the water on the alcohol burner while
she dressed.

The tea settled her, she said, after making love, and "It only takes a few moments of your time." It annoyed me, the whole tea process. I would lie on my back, hands behind my head, pleasantly lunched and napped and cuttingly impatient to get her the hell out of there and over to the Sorbonne to her library job so I could get on with my work.

"It's an insult that you never want to talk to me about painting," she would say. "I'm not stupid, you know."

"There's nothing to say. It's nothing to talk about."

"Will you have some tea? There's more water."

"Do I ever have tea? I hate tea."

"It's very good for you."

"I'm not sick. I don't need something to be good for me."

She would sit on the side of the bed then and slowly sip her tea and I would stare at the ceiling and wait. At last she would carefully rinse her cup and saucer, put them and the alcohol burner away in the armoire, slowly pull on her coat, pat and smooth her hair into place, kiss me warmly on the mouth, one long-fingered warm hand on each side of my face, and say, "A ce soir? I'll see you at dinner?" Then she would open the door, smile back at me as it closed, and leave.

She told everyone that I treated her badly, that I had no love or respect for her, that I only liked her "poosey." She spoke fluent, vulgar, and amusing English which she had learned at some knee other than mine. I did treat her badly because I was strongly drawn to her and I didn't want to be. The worse I treated her, however, the more warmth and tears and fondling and devotion she spread over me, like thick, sweet frosting on a cake.

The unpleasant fact is that, for all her attributes, she was relentlessly boring. Perhaps I loved her, I most certainly cherished her body and her mouth, her clean, sweet tenderness, her patience, her cooking, her religious attention to the mending of my clothes. But oh, sweet Christ, she was boring.

She spoke three or four languages and as far as I was able to tell, she was boring in each of them. Kind and warm and generous, passionate to a fault if such a thing is possible, considerate and giving. But all these graces vanished when she talked. She became tiresome. And (fatal flaw department) she loved to talk more than anything. "Talk to me, swittheart. Why don't you talk to me?"

Making love, she did not talk. She wasn't quiet but at least she didn't talk. Consequently we were in bed most of the time we spent together, and she thought I was a very passionate fellow. In fairness to Anna I must say that she was the most delicious and satisfying physical woman in the world (in my world, at least, past or present). Nevertheless, I am sure I would have taken less frequent refuge between her legs if the thought of talking with her had not been so boring.

She could find a day's conversation in one corner of a Matisse. At home in bed after a concert at Salle Pleyel, she insisted on discussing the program, the audience, the pianist. She wanted to compare him with last week's pianist (she devoured concerts and recitals) and project him against her knowledge of the artist who would appear next week. As my sleep-drugged head twisted toward the wall, she would throw out desperate bait – "How can you see anything in Malevich?" or "I hate all of Gauguin except the wood cuts." She would wait a few moments for a reaction and getting none, she would say, "You bastard, sahn of a beetch," turn on her side, put her arms around me, and go at once to sleep.

She loved Hofer, not as a man, but as a body of articulate opinion and more than that, as a patient, nodding, half-drunken set of indulgent ears for her endless aesthetic drivel. In exchange for one hour of Zadkine dissection, Hofer would douse her in two hours of Milhaud and a fast ten minutes of Stravinsky. She would counter with Dubuffet. Then a full gainer and a back flip into Beckett. On into and through the night with me sleeping soundly and unenlightened in a dark corner, away from her hushed intensities and Hofer's guttural counterpart. At dawn, he would totter out on cognac-deadened feet for a medicinal stop at the first laiterie on rue Vavin where he would gulp a liter of cold milk and, partially renewed, weave along the edge of the Luxembourg gardens to the cathedral St. Sulpice where he would sit in a dim corner pew, head cocked and sausage fingers conducting the organ selections, through the first two services of the morning. As soon as he left our room Anna would slip into the bed-hollow beside me, serene and fulfilled.

One afternoon she showed me the armband she had been forced to wear after the Germans occupied Paris, a yellow felt band with the word *JUIF* in black letters sewed on it. And her identity card from that time, stamped in red with the same word. And snapshots of her brothers, machine-gunned in Poland, and her mother and father, gas-chambered in a camp in Bavaria. And a picture of herself, age thirteen, looking beautifully twenty, standing with two young men in a street in Cannes, all holding Free French rifles, wearing khaki trousers and boots.

In our first naked days together, I asked her if she had ever had a baby. "Why do you ask that?" she said.

"Because I think you have." My naïveté at that time, my lack of exposure to naked breasts other than those of pink and white mid-western girls, made me conclude

179

that Anna's dark nipples must have darkened after a pregnancy, after childbirth. "You're very smart," she said, not realizing (her nipples had surely always been brown) that I had used inaccurate evidence to reach an accidentally true conclusion.

"It wasn't much of a baby," she said. Premature. Dead at birth. We never discussed it again but I always felt it had happened during the war when she was in the south with the hard-eyed young men carrying rifles.

A regal-looking girl. Not a girl really. A woman since a long time before I met her. But somewhere inside still a child (crying out in the night for *maman*), not yet either a girl or a woman. But very regal, with flat brown sculptured cheeks glowing pink without rouge, amber eyes, full, dark, unpainted lips and an arching beautiful surprise of an elegant nose. And brown, lustrous hair, straight and thick, pulled into a soft knot or hanging to her hips in the early morning, covering her straight shoulders and draping across her small breasts as she moved about the room collecting her clothes, dressing, looking out the windows, heating coffee water on the alcohol stove.

Severe clothes. Men's slacks, men's sweaters and shirts, sneakers. But girlish surprises, too. Lacy blouses, earrings, cologne, the look and smell of a woman. And always very much a woman inside the clothes.

She took me to a party one night on a rich, tree-choked street near the Etoile. She wore a dress, rare for her, and I wore a blue suit, relic from my Chicago life. It was an intimate, exquisite party. Only twelve or fourteen guests. Servants in alert attendance with cocktails and champagne trays, a roast turkey on a long sideboard, a loin of roast beef, a baked ham and salads. And bottles of pernod and cognac and whiskey scattered about on tables.

I, the frontier American, drank too much too quickly,

180

gorged myself with food (in my jacket pockets next morning, I found seven pieces of chicken which I had stored there, nakedly and greasily, for future snacks) and was loud, heavy-handed, and unappealing.

Quite late, everyone dissolving in an alcohol solution, kissing, fondling, whispering, feeling, promising, and squeezing, I went to the toilet, leaving Anna dancing a labored tango with a blonde, body-odored beauty from Stuttgart. When I came back, walking on ping-pong balls, I found them stretched out on the couch, belly-to-belly and mouth-to-mouth, being paid little notice by the others. The husband of the German blossom, a door-knob tycoon, eventually wedged them apart, but not out of embarrassment or jealousy so far as I could tell. He was simply trying to recall the name of a play that he and his wife had seen two weeks earlier in Berlin and he needed her memory.

Anna got up then, smoothed her hair, came over to where I was sitting, and resumed her kiss, this time on my mouth. I found her impaired or diminished in no way whatsoever. "Watch your step," call the hecklers, "he's a pervert!" Not so. I am only queer for women which is no perversion at all. If someone should say, "Beware of this open-faced, straightforward bastard," I would answer, "No defense. Think what you will." If my leanings were in the direction of old ladies, nymphets, middle-aged dogs, or whatever, I like to think that I would feel as guiltless in that area as I do in my present one. Being in the sexual majority (it *is* still the majority, isn't it) doesn't make me condemn the splinter groups.

181

CHAPTER THREE

All this relates (in case you're sitting, head-in-hand wondering – where in hell has he wandered to, where has he gone, where is the order he speaks about?) to the time when Anna came back from Canada unannounced and unprepared-for and met me that afternoon on the hotel stairs with Urda.

From that day until I left Paris nearly a year later, Anna, who was still my friend and occasional lover after Urda went back to Sweden (in tribute to her warm heart, Anna never turned me away when I came to her door, late and drunk), spoke freely around the *quartier* that thanks to her heartbreaking experience with me, she had become a lesbian. She also said this to me several times, usually when we were in bed and the action of the moment seemed in my mind, to contradict her words.

So what the hell? Should I have been disturbed by her damnation of me? I think not. Anna always liked women a little or more than a little or somewhat or you name the degree. She wasn't kissing that German girl because of the festive season or to show her that she forgave Germany for what had happened to her parents. No. There's a delicate theme in her concerto that plays that way; it undoubtedly always did and always will in spite of me or her husband or her kid or anybody else. So who gets hurt? Let the lovely orphan girl sleep tight and not cry "maman" in the night and eat well and raise a bright strong son and paint pictures that please her and enjoy herself in bed with whomever she damn well pleases.

Are you ready for the snapper? The story of who did what to whom with what? I said she was in many ways a bore and I didn't give her much time or let her drink her God-damned tea in peace or anything very nice and you're surely thinking that she sounds like a first-rate woman, attractive and gentle, and she deserved better treatment and that I really did, in spite of my intricate self-justifications, behave towards her like a fourteen-karat bastard. Poor little thing. Poor regal beauty. Gentle and kind and an orphan in the storm. Not totally true.

Eight months we had been together. Since ten days after Erica packed her souvenirs from Oberammergau and her kodachromes of Pisa and Rapallo along with enough Swiss chocolate to last her through her Atlantic voyage, waved and kissed and wiggled her teary, childish, Gare de l'Est goodbyes and rolled off for Le Havre, New York, Denver and daddy dear – home in time for Thanksgiving.

"Daddy says," Erica wrote from New York, "I look just like I did when I left a year and a half ago, only prettier." That pea-brained ignoramus, her old man, happy now, his baby back home. After six months of wholesome bicycle touring and a full rich year (one miscarriage and one abortion while she tried to learn the mysteries of a diaphragm) with me, the baby was flying back to Daddy-bird and the family nest in Denver, back among the upper middle-class nitwits. "Daddy will buy us a lot in the mountains."

Eight months with Anna. Good as I have described. Bad and boring also as I have described. But a unit existed there – smooth and beautifully sculptured after the filmy, unreal pas de deux with Erica.

So April came. And May. I was in and out of the

hospital in Neuilly with a painful, blood-and-pus series of infections and blood posionings that threatened to get me crated up permanently but didn't. And Anna had to leave for Canada. She had been sent there as a displaced person at the end of the war and for some idiotic, ball-breaking reason of international screw-up, she – Polish, Russian, French mixture – European resident all her life, was saddled suddenly with a Canadian passport. So she had to go there to have it renewed at four-year intervals.

"I'll only be gone a month or so," she said.

Just as she was leaving or about to leave I got a telephone call (I was fresh out of the hospital, pale and wobbly as an Angora kitten) from some international busy-body (I had screwed *her* in a moment of high exhilaration after the opening of my one-man exposition six months before and had been trying to forget it ever since) who said I must meet a Swedish director she knew who might hire me for a summer's work in a film in Sweden if he liked my looks. (Do you hear that, Urda darling? A simple little nutty random phone call which, had I not been home when it came, would never have been repeated. I would not have been in Sweden that summer. We would never have said hello, there would have been no divorce for you, no wild, long-legged daughter for us. And maybe, God knows . . . ah, well.

I had lunch with the director at Lipp's and he hired me and Anna was delighted. "It's wonderful, swittheart. You won't be in Paris alone this summer. By the time you come back from Sweden, I'll be back, too." Then she left. And the following morning I got on the Nord-Express for Stockholm.

Ten days later Morganstern sent me a card from Paris. "Did you hear about Anna? She got married in Montreal."

CHAPTER FOUR

It was late in July before a letter arrived from her. It had been forwarded from Paris, then from Stockholm, then from our first location address near Göteburg, then from Nassjö where I'd gone during a production break for a visit with my mother's relatives. At last, ink-smeared and worn around the edges, the letter arrived again in Stockholm.

Anna had married Gordon Something-or-other, a sincere, slow-witted painter she had been living with in Paris when I first knew her, before Erica went back to Denver and Gordon went back to Syracuse or Buffalo or some such dreary spot.

"He had always expected I would marry him," she wrote, "and when he met me in Canada with his parents and I saw what plans he'd made, I didn't know how to say no. I didn't want to hurt him. As it turned out, I hurt him more. I left him the day after we got married. I found out I can't be with anybody but you."

I didn't answer the letter. By then there was nothing to say except, "There's a woman here named Urda . . ."

When I got back to Paris in November, Anna wasn't there. I found out later that her annulment was a difficult thing; they made her wait a long time. Also she had heard about Urda from someone – probably Morganstern. So she stayed in Montreal until the following August.

185

By then Urda was in Paris with me, walking in the Luxembourg gardens, eating Chez Wadja, running up the seven flights of stairs to my room. That's where we met Anna when she finally came back. There on the stairs.

CHAPTER FIVE

Does it all sound too matter of fact? I suppose so. I *am* matter of fact. I don't bleed anymore; I don't want to bleed. If I am to bleed again, I'll bleed for today, not tomorrow, and sure as hell not for yesterday or for anybody who lives in the green meadows and lavender hills of that sweet old time. Today has real dimension, tomorrow is warm already, although it's still three hours away. Nine p.m., my watch says. But yesterday and yesterday's people and whatever bags of songs and sighs and tears they lugged along with them they are dead-assed gone forever. Their footprints and claw scratches are still in the wax but the feet and claws are inert and lodged in the undangerous past unless some fool brings them to crippled half-life by soft-minded memories and might-have-beens.

Burying yesterday doesn't diminish what it was in its today state, however. Looking at long-gone yesterday people with dispassion doesn't cool the warmth that was there in that present time, does it? "Don't remind me how much you loved me yesterday," the waitress said, "and don't promise how much you'll love me tomorrow. I want to be loved today."

If today is no good, then tomorrow is questionable, and yesterday is worthless. I can say this to you, my friend, because you know from a long time ago that I am a committed man, blood in the veins and warm feet. That has not changed. Don't sniff at the air for what you suspect is a sour bloodless scent floating downwind from me. My dispassionate view of scenes and people that once held me totally is today's view of yesterday. There's no other way if I am to be truthful. I can't project a rouged-up yesterday for you; no violet Seurat shadows on yellow-green grass. I can't, nor do I want to, make yesterday's people breathe again. I can't make present contact with anyone but myself and the people I love in this present – Gregg and Arthur, my mother and father, my sister and my brother. And Alicia? Yes. Of course I love her, in the way that I love, but I can't tell her that because she stitches today not only to tomorrow but to a week from tomorrow and a year from tomorrow.

And Linda? Do I still love you, Linda-baby? What do you think? When I see you during my papa-daddy visits, do you close the door after I leave, pick up the telephone and a filtered cigarette and confide to one of your D-cup, chorus-girl friends that I still love you? "He still loves me. I can tell because he never touches me, doesn't even shake my hand!" It's true. I don't. I swatted her on the rear with a folded newspaper the other morning and Gregg and Arthur and I all had a big laugh at that. And Linda laughed too. But that's not touching her.

What I want you to know is this: I have not grown old and flinty and don't-give-a-damn. I give very much of a damn. I try, however, to give less of a damn about most things. I don't want a hundred passions in my life. I want two or three, or one. I won't be nibbled by ten but I'm willing to be ripped apart by one. Is this a diamond in your eyes or a lump of coal? If coal, burn it and warm yourself. The wind is blowing like hell here. There's snow and rain outside and a milk carton burning crisply in the fireplace. And I'm for bed.

CHAPTER SIX

There's nobody here but me. Me and my things. The brushes, pens, pencils, gold fountain pen (gift from the sponsor when I was a guest on a Hollywood panel show four years ago. There was a gold pencil, too, since lost), paper clips, paper, desk diary (my accountant forces me to keep it for financial records – helps him cheat more honestly on my tax return), rubber cement, scotch tape, ink, etcetera.

There is also a fireproof aluminum portable file. Closes like an overnight case and can be easily carried by its handle providing the clasp doesn't give way and send one's documentary life whirling and blowing through the Fourteenth Street subway terminal or the Fifth Avenue bus or the wet slush of Hudson Street or wherever else I happen to be in my nomadic transferral processes.

Categories in the file are Correspondence: Personal (very thin, I burn personal letters), Correspondence: Business (very fat, business is poor but correspondence about it is excellent), Bank: Me (specified thus because there was, until recently, a folder just behind this one labelled Bank: Linda).

The next folder is Contracts, Vouchers: A study of this tangle would show anyone who was curious my income for last year, salary and billing I got for specific shows, vouchers from the Screen Actors' Guild showing residual

189

payments for re-runs. Contracts with theatre operators, withholding tax slips, and various other items of theatrical and television garbage. Also a listing in this file of the paintings I sold last year. Nine. Most pictures I've ever sold in one year.

Stocks and Bonds, Insurance (Insurance policies still there. Stocks and bonds signed over to Linda along with all other worldly goods. When I get divorced, I get *divorced*), Notes (reminder notes, legal notes, social notes, cryptic scrawled notes) and telephone numbers and addresses without names which no longer have meaning but have somehow escaped the fireplace.

Also detailed messages of advice and counsel from me to myself, a habit from my days in Europe. Reminders and nudges and guideposts written down and expanded sometimes into three-page sermons about states of mind, problems and their solutions, future goals and possible routes to them.

Since I know the clarity of your thinking, I would not recommend this kind of intellectual carpentry to you. For me, however, trapped more often than not in a maze of multiple choices and gray enigmas, this elimination of less fruitful leaps and journeys by simply crossing them out with a pencil has, on many occasions, given me fresh heart, strong legs, and a readiness to get on with it.

Fan Mail and Fan Photos: Portraits of the artist as a young cowpoke. Eight-by-ten or postcard size. Plus cards and letters from the pure-in-heart illiterates requesting them. Excerpts – "We are two found friends of yours. We have had the lucky to see you play in several motion pictures." "I watch you on television when I can. It is kind of late for me to stay up." "Please, sir, could you send me a picture? I sure will aprea it. I think your wonderful." "I am ten years old . . ." "A friend of mine said that the

190

reason I haven't seen you on TV lately is because she saw you get killed in a show last year. Is that true?" "I would like to start a fan club for you. If you would like me to boost you to the top it would be a pleasure."

The last two file folders are Automobile (containing owner's certificate for my aging but still powerful white convertible now stored in a garage in Santa Monica, rust accumulating on its radiator, dust on its upholstery, tires going slowly flat, battery running down. Also containing auto insurance policy and other miscellaneous auto-related documents), and Taxes (invoices, bills, cancelled checks, forged documents, fake signatures, and whatnot to enable me to put my best foot forward at tax time).

In the front of the file, willy-nilly, are envelopes, air-mail stationery, an astrology guide (gift from Linda when she was trying to shape me up with whatever help she could get – from the planets or elsewhere), six books of blank checks, and a small well-worn leather album crammed with pictures of Gregg and Arthur. I try not to look at those photographs every day but I can't help myself.

I have three pieces of carelessly matched luggage plus another of Linda's, borrowed, and a fifth (see above) of Alicia's also borrowed. Under the bed is a small cardboard carton with twenty or thirty tubes of oil paint inside. Fifteen are good colors, the others I will probably never use. I bought the lot inexpensively from a hard-faced father in Burbank whose son had decided to give up painting on a Friday (he was forty-five years old and a hopelessly inept painter) and had shot himself dead Saturday evening while his parents were barbecuing hamburgers in the back yard. When I bought the colors and heard the story about the son I also bought several half-finished canvases which I later painted over. In fact the only painting I have now is done, I think, on one of those canvases. Yes, it is. I just got up to look at the back of it. And a cheap piece of worthless cotton rag it is. Unlike the fine linen squares that I sweated and struggled over last year which are now, face to face and back to back, in Linda's storage lots somewhere.

CHAPTER SEVEN

Then there's my wardrobe. Tools of my performing trade. Last spring, at Linda's insistence, I bought two new suits in Westwood Village. I still have those suits plus two others I bought seven years ago plus a nine-year-old suit now hanging in Alicia's closet. I plan to have this one re-tailored. Should last nine more years.

Sport jackets. A black corduroy one in a garment bag in California, nine years old, a gift from Dort. Also a gift from Dort, same vintage, is an excellent brown tweed jacket loomed in Scotland which I wear when I do not want to look like an actor. There's a seven-year-old expensive blue blazer, gift from Linda, and a gray tweed sports coat bought by me six years ago on Vine Street in Hollywood. In Alicia's closet are two raw silk sport jackets which I bought in Beverly Hills five years ago for a personal appearance weekend in Salt Lake City.

Sweaters. A black turtleneck from England. Ten years old. Four cashmeres from five to seven years old. And a few other miscellaneous sweaters in California. Very well-fixed for sweaters.

I have fifty ties of which I wear four or five, all gifts from Linda. A black knit, a black silk, navy blue silk, pale grey silk, and light blue silk. I wear a grey wool tie if I'm looking like a painter or a red silk on Chistmas or Valentine's Day or if I feel like getting drunk and disorderly.

I look like an ape in a hat. Everybody does. I have only one hat, a tweed hat, given to me by Luther who is a serious hat wearer. When I was kidding around in California, I used to wear a green felt crew hat with "Speak Softly" embroidered on the front. Last time I saw it it was in the trunk of my car underneath the jack handle. No more green hat. No more of that life now. Bare-headed and serious now.

I have one topcoat, a gray plaid one. Linda and I picked it out in downtown Los Angeles just before we got married. She felt that a pale tan cashmere with white buttons was the thing, but I said not for a big bastard like me and she said all right, dear. But she never liked the coat I bought.

Alicia is not wild about that coat either. Square shoulders, she mentioned. Set-in sleeves. "I like set-in sleeves," she says. My coat has raglan sleeves. Accustomed to the executive look, she really doesn't like any of my clothes. Except my tight gray pants. I don't say that in a dirty way. She sincerely likes the cut of those trousers.

I am well fixed for raincoats. I have my war surplus ski-trooper weather coat which I've had for twelve years. An excellent coat. The story of its beauty, its durability, its adventures on my shoulders, has yet to be told. I wore it in a play last year and it eclipsed me.

My best raincoat is a British model with a plaid lining. It is seven years old and is in excellent condition still, except for a stained collar and beginning-to-fray cuffs. Also it needs to be weather-proofed again. The day I bought this coat was the first day that Linda ever saw me. She was trying to hail a taxi and I whistled one down for her. I don't remember that incident but she says it happened.

Shoes. I have too many. I am torn between the pain of throwing them away and the boredom of carting them around each time I move. Recently I got rid of the straight black Oxfords I bought in London during the nutty, strangely heart-rending two weeks that Urda and I spent there together.

When I think of those London days, those events, the people we saw, I can't recall what I might have said or thought, what impression I might have given or who indeed I *was* then. I do remember that I was in such a state from liquor, benzedrine, and sleeping pills and from some unnamed anxiety that has never yet clarified itself, that Urda sat one night across the table from me with untouched food growing cold between us and tears sliding down her cheeks. When I asked her, "What's happening to me?" she said, "I don't know, I don't know."

We squeezed everything into those fourteen days. We sang and laughed, drank in the pubs, and haunted the theaters. We wandered in the parks in the morning, and through Soho late at night after the theater. And one afternoon, a crisp, sunny, autumn day, we turned hand-in-hand into a bright shoe store and I bought the black Oxfords.

Tan desert boots. Very grey and dirty-tan now. A splendid gift from Dort that April when I bounced dully, like a dead tennis ball, from Le Havre to New York. Nine years ago. Dort saved me in many ways that spring, saved me in many sweet, attentive and warm ways. Although I didn't need her any more, I was very glad she was there.

The fact of her husband was no fact at all to me. I gave no damn for him or his rights or his marriage contract. She had been in my bed when he was still picking olives or contracting for olive-pickers or whatever untalented Greek monomaniacs do. I would have screwed her in front of three cameras and personally run the film for him in his private projection room for all his presence

195

in the world as her husband meant to me. He was zero. It wasn't his existence that prevented my taking her back. I just didn't need her anymore.

But I needed something. And until I could find out who or what it was, I had Dort. That was important. I see now how important it was.

In California, in the trunk of my car, are a pair of black slip-on shoes, six years old and too tight. Also my brown soft-leather (badge of my odd profession) cowboy boots. They, too, are in the car trunk. My body, I think, would fit neatly in that trunk. If not, it could be halved.

CHAPTER EIGHT

My agent calls. Would I like to do a play in Australia? I don't mind. It depends on some preliminary research on the part of the Australian producer to determine how well-known I am there from my television work. "Known and scorned, you fool. Known and found wanting."

There are other possibilities as well, agent says. Perhaps a daytime television show for the drowsy housewife audience. Would I be interested in that? I don't mind. Then there's the possibility of a tour in a four-year-old comedy playing second banana to a well-preserved (health foods and plastic surgery) sixty-year-old pederast from film-land. It's a long shot, of course, because I'm much younger than he is. And taller. And he's known to be sensitive in these areas. But would I be interested if those problems can be straightened out? I don't mind. The play we had such hopes for has, as you know, been pushed back to the fall. But if nothing else develops, you can always do a tour of the regional theaters for eight or nine weeks this summer. Shall I start investigating just in case? I don't mind. Meanwhile, there's always your State of California inter-state unemployment compensation. Yes, there's always that. Goodbye, dear agent. See you soon.

Alicia calls. The telephone is busy today. How am I? Did I sleep well? Yes, did she? Fairly well. She doesn't sleep as well, she says, when I'm not there. Sweet. If true.

Am I drawing or painting? Is my work going well? Not very well, thank you. I should get out in the fresh air, she says. It's a lovely, sunny day. I was out, early this morning. Bought the newspaper and wasted over two hours reading it. That's one reason the work goes not well. Will I be on time tonight? I hope so. Will I have to leave very early in the morning? Yes, love. It's trip-to-Fordham-Road-day to see the boys. Oh, I see. Conversation peters slowly out.

Alicia, dear child, has a burr under her blanket. "You're sweet to me and you spend time with me and you sleep with me but I'm not really important to you, am I? You could leave for California or London or God-knows-where on a week's notice and that would be that as far as I am concerned. It's not that I'm dying to get married, I know how you feel about that, but it's difficult to just keep going, smiling and happy, without knowing where you're going or if you're going anywhere at all."

"You're playing results again, Alica." Actor talk.

"I knew you'd say that, but I don't care. I want to be able to look ahead a little further than tomorrow or the day after."

She can't look ahead, of course; she realizes that. She has since the beginning because we talked about it, calmly and objectively, the first week we were together. But realizing it is one thing and accepting it is something else. So we go on, the first flood over, the current still strong but beginning now to eddy and whirl back up sometimes. More for her than for me. In my pragmatic cocoon, I find the same hedonistic joy with her that I found at first, diluted only when her troubled dissections become too sharp-pointed for either of us to ignore. When that happens we stop, strip away the bruised flesh before it starts to decay and kiss our way back into the warm meat where life still quivers and today is enough. We can still do that. At least we have been able to so far. But the dissections are getting more frequent, the probings hit more nerves, and her tiptoeing along the edge of an ultimatum is now almost constant. She won't give the ultimatum, however, because then I would have to tell her that I'm not really there in the sense that she wants, that I haven't been all along, and that I won't ever be there, anchored and committed, for anyone else again. She knows this and has accepted it, but she is unwilling or unable to admit to herself that she has accepted it. She keeps shaking her tattered little ultimatum toy, pretending to herself that an evening or a Sunday afternoon or a late night after dinner will come when she will fling it at me with a hard-eyed terrier bark that demands *oui* or *non*.

"If you only understood how a woman feels," she says, not tearfully but very simply. Inside her black-thatched head she senses, however, that I *do* understand how she feels. If I understood better how she feels she would want me less.

Hofer on Tennyson:

"Woman is the lesser man . . ." is foolishness.

If a woman is a woman at all, she's no man at all.

She's a woman. And who wants to change that?

CHAPTER NINE

Jesus, but I'm floating today. Clear out in the damp gray nothing middle of nowhere. Stare at the wall for a while. Stare out the window. Mop the bathroom floor. Sit down again. Tap the fingers. Get a glass of water. Take vitamins. Brush teeth. Take a leak. Sit down again. Clip nails.

Finally, I get up and walk down four flights for the mail. Back up. Letter from home. The high school team is heading for the state championship, they say. Two birthday cards. Tomorrow is my birthday. I haven't selected an age yet. Must consult agent. Eat? Why not? Into the kitchen where I quickly put together a braunschweiger, mayonnaise, and tomato sandwich on wholewheat, a tall glass of coffee with milk. I eat the sandwich standing up in the kitchen, drink the coffee, rinse the plate, the glass, the spoon, the knives under the faucet and put them neatly in the drainer. Now what? I sit again. An activity presents itself. I rip open the electricity bill addressed to absent landlord. Delinquent! Naturally. That's the way things are going. Service to be discontinued in five days. A muggy problem worthy of today's muggy brain.

Alternatives come slowly forward. I will go to the post office, send absent landlord an airmail letter, bill enclosed, suggesting that since our agreement did not provide for my paying utilities will he please send a check airmail special delivery to the power company so I won't find myself living by candlelight with tainted braunschweiger and clabbered milk in the hot refrigerator. Five days, however, is a short time for a letter to go to the coast and an answer, check enclosed, to come back. Now what?

I will pay the bill. I will write a check for the full amount, thirty-one dollars and sixty-four cents, and mail it, well under the deadline, to the power company. I will then send the bill stub with a note to absent landlord pointing out that I have paid to keep the lights burning. Will he please, now, pay me? What if he refuses? Or what if he doesn't refuse but just postpones, pleading temporary poverty or some such? Mightn't I be left holding the thirty-one dollar and sixty-four cent bag? Not likely, my friend. I could threaten to sell his high-fidelity apparatus, pawn his clothes, fink to the police about his illegal nickel slot machine sitting in the corner with lemons, oranges, and cherries (a loser) showing. Not likely that he'd swindle wary and tenacious me. But it could be tiresome getting my money back.

A fresh look at the bill. Could that amount be for just one month? Could I have used so much electricity? Gray, dark winter, lights on in the daytime. But still, it's too much for one month. What might landlord's reaction be?

Dear Tenant:
Although I agreed to pay utilities, I had no idea that your light bill for one month would be thirty-one dollars and sixty-four cents. Do you sleep with the lights and television set on all night? Plus the electric skillet. This is exorbitant and I will not pay it. And if you touch my high-fidelity apparatus or my clothes or fink to the police about my slot machine, I'll have you mugged.

Yours truly,
Absent Landlord

Perhaps before writing or paying, I should call the power company service representative to inquire about the number of months covered by this bill. Good plan. Hello, I'd like to inquire abut a threatened cancellation of service. Name, please. My name wouldn't help you. I'm sub-letting here. The bill is addressed to absent landlord. We must have your name, too. Why – if it's not my bill and you have no records for me? Company policy. I see. Very well, my name is Christopher Robin. R-O-B-I-N. That's right. And what is that account number? One two five dash six seven dash three two one zero dash one two one six dash four three nine! One two five dash six seven dash three two one zero dash one two one six dash four three nine? That's right. Thank you, sir. Now what is your problem? I don't want the lights turned off. Then you must pay your bill. It's not mine, it's landlord's bill. Then *he* must pay it. *That* is the problem. You see, he's in California and I'm afraid that before I can write to him and he can mail a check to you, the weekend coming on and all, the service will be discontinued. That's right, service will be discontinued if payment is not made. How about an extension? How's that? I say an extension, giving more time to pay. That can only be granted after a written request by Mr. Landlord. But he's in California and getting the request would take as long as getting the check. That's true. By then I'd have no lights. That's true. All right, I guess I'll have to pay it myself. By the way, can you tell me how many months the bill covers? Yes. Just hold the phone a moment, please. She puts the receiver down. Gay laughter and other coffeebreak sounds are heard. Five minutes pass. A man's voice says, may I help you? Who is this please? Never mind, just don't break the connection. Original lady comes back. Hello, Mr. Robin? There's no payment due

202

on this account. What? Then why are you threatening to discontinue service? Disregard that notice. We were paid four days ago. But this bill was just mailed yesterday. Well, it takes us five days to post our cash. Five days to post your cash? That's right, sir. Uh-huh, I see (click).

I look at the wall again for a while. Then at my watch. Eleven-thirty. At least I killed fifteen minutes. Should I call gloomy Alicia? Not now. Later. I doctor my deodorant burn. I glance through yesterday's paper and find the astrology prediction for today. "Be retiring and patient if relations with others appear strained today. Wait until evening for visiting or traveling about. Defer correspondence." I fish in the bookcase for landlord's astrology manual and turn it to today's prediction. "Do not venture out if you feel you may be exposed to seasonal ills or occupational hazards. Use the phone and postal mediums."

I could eat again. That would kill some time. But I'm not hungry. Braunschweiger is very filling. I don't suppose I'll be hungry enough to eat again for another hour or so. Perhaps I'll fry some eggs then. Or open a can of Norwegian sardines. Or another sandwich perhaps. We'll see.

This afternoon I'm going to see Gregg and Arthur. After I come out of the subway like a bat from a cave, I'll go to an ice cream store and buy vanilla ice cream, some chocolate ice cream, and four chocolate cupcakes with cream in the center ("They're my best cupcakes" – Gregg). Then I'll go on to their apartment. Linda will put a candle in the center of each cupcake and the four of us will sit around the table, blow out the candles, and eat ice cream and cake together. Just like a regular family. A birthday party for daddy. Isn't that a kick in the ass?

Linda and I talked on the phone yesterday afternoon to

make plans for today. A long laughing conversation. Like two lovers, I thought, after I hung up.

Last spring after she had started to talk seriously about separation but when I still believed it would never happen, I said to her one late afternoon, light-hearted, martini-in-hand, "We'll get a divorce and you can marry some wealthy, distinguished old gentleman who worships you and can support you lavishly. Then you can visit me three or four times a week for hokey-pokey purposes."

"That's a deal," she said, laughing and raising the martini glass. We were joking of course but I think perhaps she meant it. Perhaps she still means it in a non-overt, unrecognized way. Someday she'll touch me or I'll touch her and the whole intricate tableau we had together, that was perhaps the best and maybe the only thing we had, will curtain-rise again with full orchestra, corps de ballet, and colored gelatins rotating slowly. And Linda and I will be off singing in another season. The jester finished his tale of fantasy, shook his bells, waved his arms, stamped his feet and, smiling, fell dead.

Ah, well, it passes the morning at least. I almost started to focus. Now I'm staring again.

CHAPTER TEN

Linda, in her rare reflective moments away from the telephone, still tells herself, I'm sure, that though the action, the flight to Mexico, was hers, the real desire to be done with it and the drive for the crisp, unmarital air were mine.

"*You* mentioned it first," she shrilled at me those last weeks. "That's when I knew it was over, when *you* mentioned it."

I did mention it (not first, however; her dry-sherry breath carried the word almost daily during the two years in Malibu) on the plane a year ago last Christmas after two weeks with my family, a holiday made miserable by sickness and Linda's inner need for chaos.

We sat in a cramped, low-flying, two-engine plane heading for Kansas City, the boys squirming, Linda railing against my family, my profession, the plane, and the season, flying in general, and me in particular.

"You don't need me. You don't need anybody. All you really want is to be shut up in a dingy hole somewhere so you can think your beautiful thoughts and do your precious work." At last, a once-tuned, now discordant string twanged inside me.

"Linda, if everything is so lousy for you, why don't we just give up? Why don't you get a divorce?"

"That's what *you* want, isn't it?"

"It's *not* what I want. But if you're miserable all the time, if nothing gives you any joy any more . . ."

"I'm not miserable! *You're* miserable!" she hissed.

"I wasn't *describing* you. I just meant that you're unhappy. You're obviously very unhappy."

"Whose fault is that?"

"I don't know. When I met you, you were miserable because you couldn't stand your family. Now, apparently, you're miserable because you can't stand me."

"I was doing all right when I met you."

"Bullshit. You were unhappy as hell. You talked about it all the time. You talked about nothing else."

"I wasn't so unhappy," she said. "At least I had some fun then."

"Did I force you to marry me? Is that what you're saying?"

"Ah, here it comes. I knew you'd say that. I chased you for two years – coast to coast. Right? I was crazy about you. I admit it. If I hadn't chased you, you wouldn't be married. You certainly didn't want to, you and your big story about having a wife in Sweden and a child. You had a child, all right, but not a wife. You'd never been married and we wouldn't be married now if I hadn't chased you. I was a fool. I can see that now."

"If I hadn't wanted to marry you, I wouldn't have, for Christ's sake. And anything that happened in my life before has nothing to do with us now."

"That's where you're wrong. It may not mean anything to you, but it means something to me. How would you like it if you found out I had a couple of kids stuck off somewhere?"

"I never lied to you about it," I said. "I told you at the beginning. I wanted to be honest with you because I knew you'd be hurt if you found out later."

"Honest? You only tell the truth about something little so you can hide the truth about something big."

"There's no point in talking if you're just trying to hurt my feelings."

"That's a laugh. Nobody ever hurt your feelings and nobody ever will. Because you don't have any. Even your sister says that."

"All right. I have no feelings. Now let's forget it."

"You can forget it if you want to," she said, "but *I* won't. You said I should get a divorce. I won't forget *that*. You go ahead and forget it. Go back to California like a big shot and leave me alone in New York with the children like some piece of dirt . . ."

"Oh, God, let's not start that again. Why did we take an apartment in New York in the first place? Tell me that. Not because I'm rich. We took it because you hated California and wanted to live in New York. That's why we took it. I don't go to California because I like orange juice. That happens to be where I make a living. You knew it would be this way. We talked about it for months before we decided. You knew I'd have to be away from you part of the time. That doesn't mean I like it."

"You like it all right. And you can have it. If you want to get rid of me, go ahead. Go on back to your crazy paintings and your old girlfriends and your other children. You don't need me and the boys."

"Look, Linda, let's stop this. I'm sorry I said what I did. I didn't mean it and you know it. It's just been a hell of a strain this last two weeks, that's all. I'm sorry. Now let's forget it."

"*You* forget it," she said. "*I* won't forget it."

If you called me a dirty bastard twice a day for two years and finally one day I said to you, "*You're* a dirty bastard," would you turn to me and say, "We can't be

207

friends any longer because you insulted me"? Could such a thing happen? Perhaps it could. Perhaps Linda and I are no longer Linda and I simply because I, worn out and raw-nerved, said to her on that cold, bleak flight to Kansas City, "Why don't you get a divorce?" It was a horse on me, my friend, and I admit it, freely and shamefacedly. And it may have been the loaded chamber in the Russian roulette game of our marriage. But honestly, not in defense of myself but in deference to clean, sweet, one-plus-one logic, I don't think so. I know, I think, I hope, the answer lies elsewhere. But what the else is and where the where, I simply don't know.

CHAPTER ELEVEN

It's a warm sunny day today. The children downstairs on Eleventh Street are jousting with broomsticks and garbage-can lids, shouting, swearing, and preparing themselves for the future.

Hofer's prayer: (he's an agnostic Baptist)
Dear Heavenly Whoever-You-Are – please give me courage and quiet, the strength to work, a sense of joy and wonder, a tender heart, and enough wisdom so that I will place value always on these things and no lesser things.

While Arthur, pale-haired and open-mouthed in yellow pajamas, lay sleeping in my bed last night, I sat in a chair against the wall and looked at him. The plan, the threat that I had hurled angrily at Linda one day last summer came into my mind again. I let it drift and float around in there for a while, then I got up, took off my clothes and hung them on a chair, turned off the lamp and crawled into bed. I lay in the dark and thought about it some more.

I will write to Los Angeles, enclosing a check for ten dollars, and ask for copies of Gregg's and Arthur's birth certificates. Then one day when the boys are spending an afternoon with me, we stroll to a neighborhood photographer's studio (there's one at Sheridan Square,

I think) and each of us ("It was a lark, Linda. A little treat for the boys") has his picture taken. Small inexpensive photographs with extra prints for Mommy.

That same day or another day, perhaps, in case the pictures take too long, we all three get on the subway, Daddy carrying the photographs and the birth certificates, and go downtown to the complex of government buildings there.

"Passports, sir?" That's right. Here's my old one. Vaccination certificates? Jesus, I forgot all about smallpox vaccinations. Can that be hidden from Linda? Not a chance. I'll just have to bull it through. Is there a doctor near here? Two blocks away. Thank you. We'll be back later with the certificates. Boys, we're working on a surprise for Mommy. So don't tell her anything at all about what we're doing this afternoon. All right, Gregg? All right, Arthur? Good boys. But how do I explain the vaccination marks on their arms. She's sure to see them. Ah-hah. How about this?

"Linda, this story is so wild you probably won't believe it, but so help me, it's the truth. This morning, the boys and I walked up to the big post office on Christopher Street to get some airmail stamps. Then we walked over to the Hudson River to look at the ships.

"Naturally, in about ten minutes, Gregg had to go to the toilet. And as soon as he started talking about it, Arthur began moaning that he had to go, too. As you know, it's pretty bleak over there. A little on the rough side. We were too far from my place to make it home in time, so I started looking for a bar that we could go into to use the toilet.

"I found one all right, but as we were crossing the street towards it, a guy came stumbling out holding his head in his hands with blood running down from the corner of his mouth. So I thought, Jesus, I'd better not take them in there. By this time, they were both whining and clutching at themselves and hopping around from one foot to the other. So we went to the next doorway up the street from the bar and turned in there.

"It was a scroungy lunchroom with a counter and three booths, a dirty-necked, tough-looking bastard behind the counter and a greasy woman with a couple of pinch-faced kids sitting in the back booth. She was peeling potatoes.

"As soon as I go inside the door the man said, 'Yeah?' and I said, 'Three cups of hot chocolate,' and kept on walking to the back of the place where there was a dingy sign saying, *Hombres*.

"Gregg and Arthur and I squeezed into the toilet, not much bigger than a phone booth, and filthy, and I unzipped and unbuttoned and pulled and fished and steered and aimed and cussed and shook and zipped and sweated till I got them drained and rearranged. Each of them peed about six drops but the whole process must have taken ten minutes.

"When we came out finally, a shade had been pulled over the front door, there was a lot of hysterical Spanish coming from the man behind the counter, the woman and the two kids were gone, and two men in overcoats were standing by the door. One of them said, 'Oh, Christ,' as we came out of the can. Then he walked over to us and said, 'What the hell are you and those kids doing in here?' 'Going to the toilet,' I said. He asked how long we'd been in the place and I said about ten minutes and he said, congratulations, we'd just made it in time because the place was quarantined. Smallpox.

"I explained that Gregg and Arthur were my boys but that you had custody of them and they were due home in a couple of hours. The man said, 'A quarantine is a quarantine.' I kept on talking though and finally he said, 'Did you eat anything in this joint?' I said no, nothing at all. So he stared at me for a minute, walked back up front and talked with his partner, then he came back and said, 'All right. Here's the address of the main branch of the City Health Service. I'll let you leave on one condition, that you put these kids in a cab and get them over there and vaccinated right now.' He took my name and address and said he'd be checking with the Health Service later and if I hadn't been there, he'd have me arrested. I didn't have much choice so we all went and got vaccinated. Me, too."

Would Linda believe such a tale? Probably. The thought of my being pushed around by the health officers would please her. She would want to believe it. She would laugh very hard at that part. And would she connect the photographs taken previously with the vaccinations now? I don't think so.

So far so good. Passport in the works. To be mailed to me in ten days. Next step.

"I won't be coming to see the boys for a week or two, Linda. I have to go to Mexico. Have to see about a film to be shot there next fall." She envies me the trip.

I go, not to Mexico, but to Peru. Lima. I have been writing for the past few months to Wayne Booker, a high-school friend, who for five years has been head of American Express in Peru. He meets me at the airport and drives me to his home on the outskirts of the city where I meet his wife and children. We eat dinner, sip cognac and have a serious talk. Schools, language problems, extradition laws, rates of exchange, local salaries, politics and social life. I ask questions and he answers.

Finally he says, "I'm on your side, you know that. And I think you can get away with it. We will help you in every

212

way we can and as far as a job is concerned, you can work for me for as long as you want to."

We discuss salary and living allowance. Very satisfactory. Judy Booker finds me a clean, modern home, well furnished, with servants to run it and a nanny for the children. Everything goes forward smoothly. I like it here. I am liked. The Bookers have a party for me as I get ready to go back to New York. I am fizzing with hope.

Back home. Passport in my mailbox. Everything in order. Sell everything now, everything that's left. Clear the floor. Make reservations and buy tickets. Beat drums and fly banners. *Vamonos!*

"The boys missed you," Linda says. "It was nearly two weeks."

"I missed them, too. Maybe you'll let them come stay with me this week for a long weekend? I'll take them up to Woodstock."

"Of course. They'd love it. Pick them up Friday and you can bring them back Monday."

Friday morning. The boys in their dress-up clothes, their play clothes in a small bag. Anxious to be off. A weekend in the country with daddy. We go directly to the airport. "How about a little airplane ride, boys?" "I yike airplanes."

We're early at the airport. We check in, my luggage checked in the night before, have hot chocolate in the restaurant, and watch the jets land and take off. They call our flight then and we get aboard.

I look down as we circle over New York. No guilt. Not sorry.

Next day, Gregg and Arthur are playing with their new puppy in the sunny patio of our home in Lima. The Bookers and some of their friends come to visit, bringing their fresh-faced bilingual children. Gregg and Arthur play and laugh and are admired by everyone. Three days later when I come home from work, Gregg meets me at the door and says, "Como esta, Papa?"

We've made it. We've disappeared. Monday morning Linda will find my letter in her mailbox. "I'm taking the boys away. I'm sorry to hurt you but I must have them with me. I've bought a house in the south of France in the country and we'll live there. There's a good private school close by. I've bought the house under another name and we'll be using that name so don't waste money trying to find us. We're leaving the country by freighter from New Orleans; we're going by an indirect route to France. When you open this letter, we'll be three days out on the ocean. I'm sorry I have to do this to you but I cannot be a subway father for the rest of my life."

What are the problems? Could she find out by checking the airlines where I had gone? Would they tell her? Would she think of that or would she believe my letter (postmarked from Grand Central Station, to hint that I had taken a train to New Orleans) and concentrate at once, forever perhaps, on freighters and southern France? Although I am the father would I, since I do not have legal custody, be considered a kidnapper? Would the police quickly find out where I'd gone? Would they bring me back to New York? Or could I, even if found, be extradited? What's the difference? Don't count the cost. Do it!

Is it fantasy? Could I do such a thing? Could I plan it and carry it out, start it, conceal it, and finish it? Yes. Could I make a home for Gregg and Arthur and give them enough love and guidance and warmth to make up for their being away from Linda? I think I could. I would devote my life to it, my intelligence, my concentration, my heart. I know I could do it. And they wouldn't become empty, forlorn boys, lonely and unfulfilled. I'm sure I could do it.

But *would* I? Would I really, in the end, cab-to-the-airport and on-to-the-plane-and-farewell do it? Ahhh, my friend, that is *quelque chose* of another color altogether. *Would* I? God knows I could plan and arrange and adjust and find a way, somehow, to finance it. Lost in the action of the whole scheme and its execution, I could undoubtedly see it through, smooth out each fold, solve each knot, make each checkpoint, hit the marks, and carry it clearly and smoothly and professionally forward right up to the puppy on the patio in Lima.

But Jesus, no matter how strong, how secure in my decisions and actions I might be, no matter what contentment I might find in Gregg's face, or Arthur's, whatever strength and intelligence and worth I might see developing there, no matter what benefits of love and peace and solidity might result for them and for me, I could never in a million years, do it. More accurately, having done it, I could never live with it. It would grind me into the red earth of Peru or France or any other warm haven I might run to, turn me into a cold totem of self-hate in six months. Not logically or reasonably, this turning. The benefits to me and Gregg and Arthur, if I had the courage to be cruel, would be, I'm sure, many and real and lasting. I am certain of that.

But what about Linda? My whole pyramid of self-assurance and right action comes sifting down to the ground when I imagine her at the mailbox, in slacks and sweater and sleepy-eyed, looking for God-knows-what (my weekly check perhaps) and finding, like a new continent, the hard-edged world of my letter.

I could never make such a jagged incision in the softest part of her. It would leave a wound in my own abdomen

215

that no clamp or suture or length of gut could close. I could not do it. I wouldn't. I *can't*.

Random notes from Hofer:
1. To create art, forget art.
2. The shirt of guilt is made of concrete.
3. A man's life should be dedicated to the exploration of one primitive part of the universe, the wild, uncharted area that stretches from his forehead to the base of his skull, from his left temple to his right.

CHAPTER TWELVE

I took my raincoat to the cleaner this morning to be cleaned and treated with a solution to make it rainproof again. When I emptied out the pockets, I fished inside a zipper-closed pocket in the lining and pulled out a dime, a paper clip, a three-year-old receipt from a service station in Santa Barbara, and a slip of paper with the words (my handwriting), "I think I'll give it up," scrawled on it.

That trigged that? No circumstance or incident comes to my mind. I check the date on the gasoline slip but it brings no flash of history and no assurance that the same date applies also to the scrawled note. In that time of the warm marital cocoon what did I consider giving up?

Ignoring it is the easiest way. And the wisest. Who is trouble-seeking fool enough to hinge a moment or even an eyelash-flicker of time to a folded scrap of uncertain feeling felt at an unspecific moment? Not I. I push the incident out of my mind. A fascination with it lingers, however, fuzzy and warm and undangerous, like a fresh-hatched chick in my hand.

I can sense your crackling mind, bored with such shit, accusing me. I'm building from the roof down, you snarl. I admit it and I don't defend it in this instance, although I do defend, sometimes, that kind of airy construction.

About the slip of paper I know nothing further except this: It hints to me that a chord which I assumed was composed only last fall may actually have been jotted down long before that. Today's self-portrait is the crude sketch of a long time (how long?) ago. Do you see what I'm nibbling at or, more accurately, what is nibbling at me? The benevolent God-image monster I've been molding, with your eyes and ears as armature wires, is threatening to turn on me or threatening at least to be more stubborn about its destination, its route, and how much of my sullen weight it will continue to carry.

So shall I cringe, cover my eyes, and give up? Not likely. I am stubborn if not brilliant, relentless if not wise. It's my monster and I'll live with it, benevolent or no. Since I don't know my destination and since I have no assurance, furthermore, that I'll recognize it when I get there (tin whistles piping, toy drums rolling) I am not afraid to go on. At least, I have found an excellent new epitaph (unusual to find one written in the future tense), "I think I'll give it up." Lovely.

I'm on my back in bed, head propped by a folded pillow. I have been here all afternoon, windows closed, shades drawn, lying straight and heavy under warm blankets and staring. The sunlight is bright in the streets but the drapes thin it to a pale blue wash. I lie here, eyes fixed on that cool rectangle, half larva, half insect, waiting for wings – the muscles and nerves in warm suds, the brain absent in some recreation yard (jostling inside a bouncing ball?) and replaced in the cranial cavity by wads of cotton wool, wisps of straw, and shreds of excelsior. Euphoric state, past consciousness, short of sedation. Pleasant, nerveless, plug-out-of-the-socket, receiver-off-the-hook. A condition sought after, dreamed of, medicated for. Peace. Escape. Floating in the parenthetical middle-distance, free of nagging backache, smoker's hack, discomforts of the common cold, neuritis, neuralgia, and hemorrhoids. In a world of gnawed nails, chewed lips, and twitching muscles, among the gum-chewers, chain-smokers, binge-drinkers, pill-takers, foot-tappers, and dial-twisters, I lie like a quiet pool in the canyon of an afternoon with no word or thought to unsettle my flaccidness. Block on block on bright-colored block.

This catalepsy is death for me. But I can't shuck it. It exists suddenly and when its soft time is spent, it stops. But in that time, it is a tenacious entity that cannot be dissolved. If I had jumped out of bed this afternoon, taken a shower, dressed myself, strolled to the White Horse and drunk five fast steins of beer, gone to a movie, met friends for dinner, laughed and danced and drunk wine until very late, if I had come home at last half-drunk and dead-tired to fall into bed and a deep restful sleep, the end result would have been no different. When I woke up tomorrow morning, the trance would be with me as though I had never left my bed this afternoon.

Sound interesting to you? Appeal to your mystic middle? Want to buy a few shares? Take a cataleptic fix for a few afternoons to give your nerve endings a chance to heal? Forget it.

CHAPTER THIRTEEN

Urda has sandy hair. And blue eyes. She used to say to me, "We have the same colors."

We do look alike. When she first arrived in Paris, I took her to *Wadja's* for dinner and as I paid the check I said, "I'd like you to meet my sister." Madame Wadja, hair disheveled, apron stained and twisted, her eyes shining lewdly behind tiny spectacles, said loudly in French, "Sister? Yes – sister of your thighs," cuffing me in the stomach with the back of her hand and pushing me away from her cash drawer.

"What did she say?" Urda asked me when we were in the street. When I told her, she laughed crazily and said, "Ah, you see? She *knows* you. I like her." She knows *you*, I said. "Yes, yes," she said, "she knows me, too. I am the sister of your thighs. Oh, I like her so."

The child, Ingergerd, looks sweetly and unbelievably like Urda. With red hair, like both of us, and eyes like mine. After seeing snapshots of her taken at the beach (how long ago those other beach snapshots of Urda and Wade and me laughing away the innocent July time) I wrote that she seemed to be built like me.

Urda wrote back in her beautiful, less-than-perfect English, "Ingergerd is talking to me all the while, impossible to concentrate! She is impolite and egoistic and selfish! She really is. Irritating and wild and nearly impossible for me to handle. All this is true. And all the sweet and good things are true. Who can she be like? She has your building as you saw from the pictures. And your stubbornness and fighting for 'who is the strongest?'" I fight no longer, Urda dear.

Last Sunday, Alicia said to me, "I promise myself every day that I won't ask you if you love me. If you don't, I'd rather not know. If you do and don't want to say it or can't say it, I suppose I must accept that. I guess most men don't like to talk about how they feel."

I sat, glass-in-hand, looking at her and thinking, she really is a very nice woman, but thinking also that I did not belong in the niche where for reasons of generalization (men are sweet idiots) or self-preservation she was trying to fit me.

"I'm not that way," I told myself. "I told Linda I loved her every day. Often many times a day." That was, perhaps, one of my mistakes. A very drunk woman said to me once, "Love is no mystery so long as you accept the fact that it's temporary. Only unrequited love lives forever." Then she added, "Only cynics and children love well."

I feel as though I've been over this ground with a rake and a hoe and a harrow and a drill. Seventy-four times each. Wearing out the poor soil. Wearing out tractor parts, using up gasoline, and making a tractor-seat callous on my buttocks. Breathing fresh air, soaking up sunshine, but not planting anything. And sure as hell, in this season, not harvesting. But things, I keep assuring myself, will change. An orange and excellent morning will come when I laugh and scratch and shave and brush my teeth and piss a lovely arc and start something new. When it comes, my friend, your face will have an engraved reproduction of itself on that morning's brass plaque.

Letter from absent landlord. He will be away for two more months. I'll have a roof for at least sixty more days. Things clicking slowly and soggily into place. I even got forty-three dollars and sixty-seven cents refund on my automobile insurance.

I had eggs and toast and coffee for breakfast. It's warm here even with the radiator turned off. And the light is good. This is not *the* morning, God knows, but it is a *good* morning. Objects have shadows today, the sidewalk cracks are beautiful, incisive, and symmetrical, and the woman who leans, heavy-bosomed, from her window across the street, is beautiful.

There was a young woman on the Lexington Avenue subway the other evening, hanging on a strap in the crush, reading a worthless popular novel. An ordinary girl, large, brown-skinned, Italian-featured, with thick, blue-black hair. I couldn't stop looking at her hair.

You know me from long ago. I do not paw or pinch or chase. Never in the old days. Never since. Not now. But I was tempted (actually considered it – schoolboy trick) to go past my station just to see where she might get off. Would I have followed her then? I hope not and I trust not since I got off the train without hesitation when it came to my stop.

As I walked away down the platform, I looked back and saw her quite ordinary face turned down to her book and I thought as I climbed the stairs to the street, not "I wan't my arms around her," or "I want to fuck her," but, "God, won't I ever see that gorgeous hair again?"

Don't sit back and scratch your curls and say 'fetish' to me. If it were, I'd admit it and indulge it if possible. Nor do I mean that starting with love of her hair, I could

222

be alone with that girl without being drawn to the rest of her. I would be hers, I'm sure, balls and all. But the feeling was not that; it was a visceral jolt. Do you understand now? I don't want that girl, for Christ's sake. I don't want to scissor off her hair. I don't need her name, her address, or her brassiere size. But I very much want that thump-in-the-belly moment. I *need* it. I don't want to lose that till the pennies kiss my eyelids.

CHAPTER FOURTEEN

I have been treading water for too long. I must try now to joust directly with things that have needed for some time to be jousted with.

You first, Alicia. You arrived last so you come first. How long now? Five months next Monday. An easy-to-remember date, same day as the divorce. Not planned that way. I had no specific drive to be with a woman that evening, no need to symbolize the freedom of the day. But it happened. You, by chance, left your office as I was leaving an adjoining office. We, by chance, shared an elevator and you, by chance, said, "Hello again. How have you been?" I said I'd been fine and you said, "If you're a good boy, I'll let you buy me a drink this afternoon."

> The lass who hides behind her fan
> Will spend her days without a man.

Don't misunderstand, my friend. Alicia is attractive, confident, and bright. She has an interesting job plus alimony. She lives alone on a fashionable street, dresses elegantly, undresses beautifully, mixes excellent cocktails, cooks well (every night if I show up), and doesn't talk too much. She had a shattering divorce two years ago and is not over it yet. Many men choose her but she prefers to choose rather than be chosen. She has probably slept with five or six men since her divorce but does not admit this to herself. She lies to me sometimes, more often to herself. Still, with me, she has been generous and loving and much less demanding than she feels she has a right to be.

How have you fared, Alicia, in our five months together? Begin with our first meeting outside your office. You happened to pop out just as the man I had come to see walked into the reception room to get me. We were introduced. I realize now that you wander out of your office whenever you hear a man's voice in the reception area but I don't hold that against you.

You say you were drawn to me at once. I was certainly aware of you. Although this was some time before the divorce, I was already living alone in the apartment, and I wondered after I met you that day why my wife couldn't at least smile at me as you, a stranger, had. I also thought that if Linda and I should actually get divorced and if I should start having dates with new women, laughing and teasing them and undressing them the way I used to do eight million years ago, I'd like to laugh with and undress *that* woman. You. I wondered later, when divorce was truly imminent, about how you lived. And where. I surmised correctly that you had been married, incorrectly that you had a child. I wondered if there would be a babysitter problem if I should ever take you out to dinner. Or perhaps cocktails some afternoon.

The afternoon came. And the cocktails. Then a drink at your house before we went on to a party. I kissed you and you sat on my lap and I assumed I would make love to you that night. But I got drunk at the party and met a lot of people I didn't expect to meet and I almost left and went home with that wide-mouthed actress with green eyeshadow and big, creamy tits. Did you know that? She left early, you remember. She was going home to wait for me. But I didn't go. I went home with you instead and we started something that you refused to finish. "I didn't want to sleep with a drunk," you said later. So I went home and you had a date the next night and the following day was Sunday. We had breakfast, spent the afternoon in bed, and the next day I left for California.

From the beginning, I was fair and honest with you, wasn't I? No more marriage for your old cross-eyed buddy, I said. Not now. Not ever. Tried it and didn't like it. Didn't have my size in the store. Haw, haw! We had an enjoyable time discussing it. In the two weeks between my coming back from California and taking the boys to Missouri for Christmas, and all the weeks since then, I felt that our first laughing discussions, the warm and friendly you-know-me-pal, I'm-with-you, dialogues of two smooth, once-burned (once each) contestants, were a foundation for our relationship. Faring well together, I thought.

As I watched you cooking and washing dishes and worrying about my eye strain, I said (often), "You're too good to me. I'm turning you into a drudge," and you, very tough with your hands on your hips, said, "Honey bun, if I didn't want to do it, I *wouldn't* do it."

Irish mist and rum punch. Vodka martinis and Johnny Walker on the rocks, Cognac, Drambuie, and many, many bottles of Beaujolais and Burgundy. You said, shortly after Christmas (I always drink a lot at Christmas time), "Don't you think you're drinking too much?" I said no. And on my birthday, both you and Luther, ignoring my flat belly, clear eyes, and rosy cheeks, said, "You sure do drink a lot," and I said, no I don't, except on festive occasions. "Since both of you are dear friends – whenever I'm with you, it's a festive occasion." That night the three of us drank a bottle of scotch, three bottles of Medoc,

226

half-a-bottle of slivovitz, and three-quarters of a bottle of cognac. I do not drink too much. I think too much. "You'll never be happy," my sister says to me. "You think too much."

What dinners you cooked, Alicia. Flank steak, chicken livers, beef liver, hot sausages, pork chops, lamb chops, pork roast, sirloin steak, fried chicken, broiled chicken, roast chicken. And roast beef. Endive, asparagus, artichokes, broccoli, mashed potatoes, french-fries, hashbrowns. And knockwurst. No knockwurst for a long time now. Not since I burned the roof of my mouth eating too quickly so we wouldn't miss the start of the movie on Third Avenue. Coffeecake in the morning with tomato juice and black coffee in big mugs. Cheese after dinner or with drinks or at any crazy time. Brie, camembert, roquefort, munster, gorgonzola, gouda. Chocolate cake from the *patisserie*. Scrambled eggs on Sunday with crisp little sausages. Yum, yum.

In return for all this, I gave you the museums. The Frick, the Modern, the Metropolitan, the Guggenheim. I stretched your mind. And your way of seeing. Or if neither your mind nor your way of seeing are changed, certainly your attractive legs benefited. Climbing the stairs, walking the halls and the ramps, strolling Central Park and Fifth Avenue later. "He's good for my health, at least. He gets me outside, into the fresh air. He's good, I'm quite sure, for my health."

However you have fared, you can see that I have fared beautifully and happily. I am grateful for having had you warmly beside me all these wet and cold winter weeks, grateful for all the good things. Unfortunately, however, no matter how good it was, you are now screwing it up. Worse than that, you have already screwed it up. Your secret eyes, when I surprise them looking at me these last weeks, your teeth nibbling the skin from the inside of your cheeks, your fingers picking lint shreds from the back of the couch, show me that our scrap of silk is wearing thin for you. Maybe, though you can't bring an end to it, you will welcome it when it comes.

I'm not mad at you, baby. You're a lovely woman who wants to get married again. (Luther says all nice girls want to be married. True, I suppose, but a hot one coming from Luther.) Don't misunderstand me. You'd make an excellent wife. I'm sure you were an excellent wife the first time. And I genuinely want you to have what you want. I want you to be Mrs. Someone-or-other and wear hostess gowns and earrings and drive a blue sports car and have a suntan the year round. But that's one life and I'm another. I'm committed and spread around already and there's nothing left to hand out any more. Nothing permanent. I'm Urda's property. And Ingergerd's. And Gregg's and Arthur's. And Linda's too, I suppose, in some crappy way. All the space is rented and there's no waiting list. Not even a cot in the lobby.

> Goodbye, Alicia.
> Farewell, Alicia,
> Bye-bye, Alicia,
> I talked her away.

Not quite so simply, my friend. Not so simple. For lovers, words have meaning only before the beginning and after the ending. Alicia and I are past the one and not up to the other. When I take my gray suit out of her closet, the red robe from the bathroom, my slippers from the shoe rack, when I pack all these

228

things in a bag, say ta-ta, and walk out the door, into the elevator, downstairs and out through the carpeted hallway to the street, then perhaps the words will start to have meaning again. Until then we go on, unquiet and physical together.

CHAPTER FIFTEEN

To the country this weekend. To the clean air and the muddy fields, fried chicken and Dutch beer, and pale scotch by the tumbler-full. I might paint a picture if Abe has an old discarded canvas in some corner. I might also (more likely) just sit and giggle and talk Southern and drink and belch and bounce the baby girl and maybe, in a quiet bedroom moment, write a letter to Urda.

I telephoned Linda. May I visit tomorrow morning before leaving for the country? Better not. New husband is sick. Pity. We don't discuss his ailment on the telephone but last time we talked she said he was suffering from diarrhea. Still with him apparently. Too bad. Heh-heh.

Arthur, in his turn at the telephone, said, "I want to come and stay all night with you, Daddy." Daddy said not this weekend, honey, but soon. Besides, it's Gregg's turn next but I didn't tell Arthur that.

So I'll get on the train at Grand Central and go up to the country and get good and conscientiously drunk and maybe there will be some grass widows or plain widows or horny divorcees there. Or buck-toothed teenagers in tight sweaters selling Girl Scout cookies at Abe's door. If not, however, then drunk will be enough, plus food and music and the crisp air and distance from the city and a lot of loud laughing. And Abe and his wife singing, "The Wabash Cannon-Ball."

Be encouraged, my friend, because I am. The sea will part, the icepacks will melt, the meteors will cool down, and the sound of auto horns will be heard no more in the land.

The weekend passed. It was pastoral and I did not get drunk. Abe said I was drunk but I wasn't. He was. One hour after I arrived at his house, we walked to a neighbor's place nearby where a vat of maple sap was cooking in a shanty (it's Spring, for Christ's sake, already) and there beside the neighbor, lo and behold, stood two little girls holding boxes of Girl Scout cookies. I said to myself, "Very good, so far, noble seer. Now let's bring on the grown-up females." After such a beginning, I really expected that one or more would appear. But Saturday passed. And Sunday. Monday morning I took an early train back to New York and still no love object had turned up.

This is the kind of day it is today. Yesterday was the same. Head to the wall, feet to the window, sheet over the head, a warm, foggy life in the bed. Reading old newspapers, leafing through magazines, getting up to go to the toilet or to make a sandwich, then back to the silence of the bed.

There are two radios here. Neither, since I've lived here, has been turned on. In four years in Paris, I never had a radio in my room. I mentioned this with pride to Linda one time. She said, "You never had a radio in all that time?" and I said, that's right, and she said, "You're nuts." She didn't understand that I love silence. The grave must be a peaceful and marvelous place.

I may have to become a tap dancer. Judging by my steelwool headaches of the past few weeks my eyes are starting to peter out.

One day, when I was twenty or twenty-one years old,

I listed what I considered to be my major talents, there must have been at least a dozen on the list, and I vowed that I would develop each one fully so that no matter what faculty I might have to do without in the future, arms, legs, hearing, sight, or speech, I would be able to function fully and creatively in at least one area that did not require the use of the faculty I had lost. I reasoned that a singer could be blind, a painter could be deaf, etcetera. And a lover? What does a lover need? Only a lovee.

This week, astrological predictions to the contrary, has started off badly. My unemployment check did not arrive in the mail, my head aches, my agent does not call. Linda (hungover and red-eyed) barked at me yesterday morning when I went to visit the boys.

The boys, at least half the time now, call me by new husband's name instead of my own. I lost a play last week because they hired a worn-out movie queen for the lead who would have looked, on stage, like my great aunt rather than my wife as the author had indicated. Alicia is away on a ten-day holiday to New Orleans, taking both her kitchen and bedroom talents with her, I have had no mail for several days, and an old football injury to my shoulder is paining me.

Hofer (in conversation)
There is no such compound as autobiographical fiction. It does not exist. A man who takes a personal, historical position in relation to his experience will write autobiography. If he takes a fictional position – even though he reports personal experience – the result will be fiction.

CHAPTER SIXTEEN

I have accepted the fact, only very recently, that Hofer is dead. Even if there is some flicker of pulse or breathing still left in the bloat he has made of himself, he is no less dead. This acceptance won't pad the moment when I finally read or hear the specific facts and dates but it will make the after-moments less painful perhaps since they exist now before the fact and need not be lived through and bled over again.

No Hofer stumbling about in the world is a painful thought. Not because of his death but because of the waste of his life. I have a closer contact with that waste-path than I do or did with Hofer himself. This is not coldness or lack of sympathy in me. It is evidence of how much, in the twelve years or so I knew him, that Hofer came to be, in my mind, synonymous with waste.

I know no way to avoid the pain of his death. I simply have to stand here, flat-footed, hands at my sides, and take it. The thing I will not accept any longer (Linda insisted that I had to accept it) is responsibility for his life. I shuck that. It was never mine or anyone's (he tried to pass it on to everyone he knew) but his.

I accept the sorrow. But the guilt is not for me. No more. I have had that guilt with me since the summer we met on the freighter, since his squandered months in Switzerland with frequent side trips to France, since his visit in my cold apartment in New York, and since that hideous last meeting in San Diego. Each time I felt that some suggestions or scoldings from me might shape him up. After I'd lectured him and listened to him and he had gone away to wherever he was headed, I often felt that I should have been more specific, less patient with his circular reasoning. I believed it was my fault, somehow, if he went away with the cobwebs still in his mind.

People looked on him as my responsibility. In Montparnasse, the concierge of my hotel would come to me with, "Oh, *monsieur, votre ami,* Mr. Hofer, he makes such noises coming home at night." Or Morganstern, "Jesus, he's getting into a hell of a shape. Can't you tell him . . ." And Anna, "I feel sorry for him. He's like a baby. Why don't you talk to him? He'll listen to you."

So I talked and Hofer listened and nodded his head. But he kept on sliding and I kept feeling guilty. I've been wearing that concrete shirt all these years I've known him, up until this morning, this hour. Now I'm taking it off. I'm turning you loose, Hofer, You're not my responsibility and you never were. My own idiocies, my sins against myself, my home-grown guilt, that's enough for me. That's a lifetime supply for me.

I'm turning you loose, too, Linda. I'm wrapping up all the self-recrimination and soul-searching and self-hate and sending it special delivery, air mail, to whom it may concern, in care of the postmaster, Santa Claus, Indiana. No return address. If not claimed, dump it in the dead-letter office and let's forget about it. Is all that possible? Can I do it? I must.

CHAPTER SEVENTEEN

Long time lapse. Long for me. Six days.

Pistol in hand, barbiturates close by, razor blade at the ready, I resume. Don't fret about my suicide humor. If I should ever decide to empty out my rich, type O blood into some rented bathtub, I would not degrade the creative splendor of that act by hawking it about. Not only would I not burden you with it beforehand, I would take pains to see that you would be among the last to know. A suicide still warm is more painful to contemplate, certainly, than one long-cold. (I speak from the experience of my mortuary days.)

I disposed of four people last night. It had been a foggy and many-tendrilled week and I had to do it. My eyes had been burning and my throat got sore and my head clogged up and my nose started to run. It was that kind of a week.

Yesterday was Sunday, the beginning of a *new* week, and I knew that something had to be done to clear things away and help me see the go-ahead course. These four people had been disturbing me for days, some for much longer, and I decided at last that they would have to be disposed of. One of them was an old, close friend and the least of the four was a girl I had known for several years. But I had to go ahead with it, all the same.

I took a sheet of white stationery from my file box,

lettered each of the four names in large black letters on the paper. Then I dipped a sable brush in red ink and made a bloody, slashing stroke through each name. When the ink dried, I cut lengthwise with a scissors through each name, shuffled the long strips together and cut them across so that all that was left was a neat little stack of cut paper squares. I put them carefully into the fireplace, cleaned out earlier for this ceremony, doused them with lighter fluid, and set them afire. They burned quickly. I watched until the last flicker of flame, the last wisp of smoke was gone. When I looked at the black smear of ashes in the empty fireplace, I wasn't sorry. I felt relieved.

Two of the people, a man and his wife, should have been burned earlier. My ashes were in their fireplace long ago, I'm sure. I had sensed it before but never so strongly as last Thursday, in a telephone conversation with the wife. Her sweetness, her hesitations, her self-consciousness, sent her contempt showering through the phone like hot sparks.

When I came out of the telephone booth by the curb, Gregg (we were out walking together) said, "What's the matter, Daddy?" I said nothing's the matter and I took his hand while we walked on down the street and I thought, my God, have I become so hateful? What have I done to them that they should despise me so? And whatever it was, how could I rectify it?

This was my first reaction before I realized after much thought that the only solution was to burn them. No dragging it out with telephone calls and polite visits and how are your children or would you like coffee or how about a beer? No pissing around and stalling and let's be nice to each other even though you detest me. Instead let's get it over quickly. With blood-red ink and a scissors and lighter fluid and a match. Poof!

Victim number three is no great loss, I suppose, but for

236

the little I knew her I valued her. As an intelligence, at least. I met her the summer I came to New York from Europe, nine years ago last month. Tall, thin, well-bred, and honed to a fine, intellectual edge, the kind of girl I had never courted or been courted by. I used to run into her in art galleries and here and there. Two or three times she asked me to drop by her apartment for a drink but I was always occupied elsewhere and she accepted my gentle refusals gently.

One time, however, I did accept her invitation. I ran into her at a newsstand in her neighborhood and she said would I like and I said yes I would like but I could only stay a few minutes. She said fine so we had the drink and it was pleasant enough for a quarter of an hour. She said a few interesting, well-read things and I thought, "Nice girl, citizen of another world. Adieu!"

Then I ran into her last fall at the Whitney. I said, "I just got a divorce," and she said, "I just got married." She said she had been living in the Orient, writing for archaeology magazines and working spasmodically on a book of her own. She looked less arid to me than she had a few years earlier.

After Christmas I saw her again, on Fifth Avenue. She said, "It didn't work, I'm getting a divorce," and I said something worldly like "Welcome to the club." We exchanged telephone numbers and I, laved in the gentle wealth of Alicia, forgot the conversation and lost the phone number.

Early in February, she called me and said there was a party the following night, a brilliant affair, and would I like to escort her? Thank you very much for asking me, but I'm afraid I can't. You'll be sorry, she said sweetly. I'm sorry now, I said.

I *was* sorry. I had envisioned a penthouse crowded

with full-blown divorcees, lonely and with independent incomes. Also, the Alicia bridle was starting to chafe my mouth even then. But because I knew she expected me the following night, I said no to the party.

The girl, proud and undoubtedly miffed, telephoned no more. I called her a couple of times so she wouldn't think she was unattractive or that I hated her and our conversations were pleasant. But no mention of parties. Not until last week. She called on Monday and mentioned, quite casually, a casual affair, a dinner, to be held on Thursday.

I picked her up at her apartment. Gracious neighborhood. No stick-ball, no garbage in the streets, no window-sill leaners, no front-stoop sitters. Fancy. She poured me a scotch and herself a ginger ale and we talked. Actually, I talked while she (I realized later) studied me from behind her soft drink.

The party (we arrived first, bad omen) was intimate in size, British in character. Since I admire and truly like the British, I settled back comfortably, munching salted walnuts, speaking with intelligence, and some wit, I felt, sipping scotch from (thanks to the host, a self-effacing, gray-haired fellow) a bottomless glass.

There was spaghetti and cheap red wine later and I drank and ate a lot. And there were two girls. One was quite attractive (small-breasted and red-faced, but appealing) and the other was quite near. She sat beside me at dinner. My thin companion was in a remote spot at the other end of the table.

I cannot tell you the exact details of the late part of the evening. I think we were among the last to leave but I remember nothing of the leaving or of our taxi ride home. There is one clear cameo picture in my mind, when the girl turned at her door, not her apartment door but the

238

outside door of her building, and bade me a simple good night. The fact that she did not invite me upstairs is not significant. But the expression on her face as she stood there was crippling, a look of weary disillusion.

The next day was a loss. I was not ill but confused. My raincoat and my suit were hanging in the closet, an indication that I had arrived home physically capable at least. No evidence of falling on my trouser knees, no stains, other than spaghetti-sauce spatters, on my gabardine jacket. Shoes neat, on trees, in shoe bag, and still shined. Money in place in billfold. Should I feel guilty or not?

I call the girl. She is cordial, but busy. "Having breakfast with the girl across the hall." Excuse me, I've made a mistake. That was the second day after the party. The first day I called and left a message with her answering service asking her to call me. Then because my wine wounds were fresh and I was afraid of her not returning my call or of what she might say if she did, I quickly dressed and went out. A hot beef sandwich on Second Avenue and a grim double-feature movie. When I finally did speak to her it was the evening of the second day. Gregg was staying with me and would she like to meet us the next morning in Central Park? Gee, thanks, she'd love to but she had to work on an article all the next day. No mention of the party from her. "It was a nice party," I said. "I liked your friends." "Yes," she said. Just yes. I said I'd call her in a few days and she said that would be nice.

Unless I have the world's most creative guilt center, I think this may be what happened at the party. I have a feeling that something went on between me and the quite ordinary girl on my right. There may have been some nudging or knee bumping which in those close quarters seemed to be something other than what it was. Since it was a narrow table, there may also have been, probably was, a little knee action under the board with the red-faced girl who sat across from me. I really don't know. I'll never know, I suppose. And in all honesty, I can't say that I give much of a damn. Life, *my* life at least, is filled with such incidents. And who suffers? Not I. I have no need to excel or be admired at sensible little parties, no fear of becoming an anecdote in a London parlor. Let them judge me, for Christ's sake. Let the skinny girl condemn and feel superior and disillusioned and confide over toast to the girl across the hall, "You'd never expect it from a man like him. And right at the dinner table." Her judgments are no longer important to me. I burned her.

The fourth victim is another matter altogether. In retrospect, I suppose the least he deserved was to be sacrificed by himself in a separate ceremony. But it's over now. He burned with three people he didn't know and would not, I'm sure, have liked. I am a little sorry about those circumstances but, still, he got what he deserved.

I had known him since I was seven years old. We went to grade school and high school together. We played football, smoked cornsilk, and chased girls together. You may have met him. He went to Washington University in St. Louis but he used to visit me at college once or twice a year. Through thirty years of living on the same block, living on separate continents, different careers (he's a lawyer), marriages, divorce, widowhood (his wife, a girl we both went to high school with, was killed five years ago driving home from a summer-theater matinée in Westport), different politics (he is conservative-conservative and I as you know am something else), we had nonetheless kept a warm relationship, more brothers than friends. But I burned him last night. I had to.

I don't know precisely what triggered it. It had to start

240

with him however. It could never have started with me. I had made no qualitative judgment of him since age seven. I accepted him like I accept the palm of my hand. Whatever the thing was that jogged his mind, it must have taken place some time ago. Or perhaps it happened like a snap of fingers that evening a few weeks ago at dinner.

We were with two other people, a kind and decent man and his restless wife, close friend of *my* friend, casual but warm friends of mine. We had had cocktails and were having wine with dinner. It was a pleasant leisurely restaurant. We were enjoying our conversation and laughing a lot. I like to laugh.

Our friend's wife was annoyed by the success of a playwright whom she considered untalented. She was dissecting him and his work unmercifully. In the general laughter, I looked at my friend. He was looking at me strangely, the same look on his face as the thin girl had when she said good night outside her apartment building.

Later that evening I caught the look on his face again. I was alerted. Each time I saw him during the next few weeks, I studied his words, his reactions, his expressions. Superficially, the same man, the same old friend. But gradually I saw the change. A film had grown over him. He soaked up light but reflected none. His eyes when we talked now were a judge's eyes. Sometime in the past, at some moment I hadn't been aware of, he had judged me. Some judgment had been handed down and sooner or later, in his own deliberate time, he would let me know it. Since I have no desire to know it (I am determined *not* to know it) I burned him quickly with lighter fluid. And in the company of the other three.

The burning has had a strong and positive effect on me. Like a savage burning his clothes, his implements, his home even, as an act of faith in his God, himself, and his future, I burned four friends. Do you understand? There is a loving Christ and a fighting one, a God who creates and a God who destroys. One foot going straight and strong ahead, the other club-footing to a separate cadence. Dragging. But that is the way of it. *Accept* is the key word. I accept things badly. Many things I can't accept at all.

CHAPTER EIGHTEEN

Where were we? I had disposed of Alicia, the brown-skinned flower of the Caribbean or Montevideo or Paramus or wherever she's from, disposed of her kindly and completely. But only in theory. Actual disposal of the living carcass itself is another matter. Cut in two-inch chunks perhaps and scatter about the city in trash cans, wrapped in squares of aluminum foil. The skull is the problem. It fits nowhere except in the hollow of one's shoulder. Alicia's head fits so beautifully in the hollow of my shoulder that I really mustn't cut her up and aluminum-foil her or dispose of her in any way whatsoever other than symbolically. And I've done that, haven't I? Who knows?

Can you see the shoots struggling up through the openings in my skull? No blossoms yet, no fruit, no colored envelopes from the seed store even indicating what if anything will flower and bloom here. But Jesus Christ, isn't it a beautiful blessing to see anything green at all poking out of soil that just a while before was frozen and seedless?

I'm not nuts, am I? There *is* a cleared spot in the gravel, isn't there? I know that the golden morning I've been babbling on about is not coming. I realized that when I mentioned it before. But I needed it then so I used it. I need it now in a different way but it's not here now to use.

Linda, what in hell am I going to do about you?

I can't kill her. I can't ignore her or forget her or pretend she never happened. I can't even hate her. All I can do is sit and wait for the water dripping on stone to wear her away. It will happen of course. It always does, doesn't it? Maybe it has already begun.

I can look at her now. I can shake her hand, hold her arm, put my arm round her shoulders, kiss her on the cheek. I can be as cordial and patient and understanding as I would be with a stranger. This new strength should make me *feel* strong, shouldn't it? It should but it doesn't. Can you understand it? Can you understand that I would punish my brain to find some device or implement that might help me turn a still-living thing into something cold and then when the warmth finally starts to go away, that I would hate to see it happening?

I can't understand it. At least I don't understand all of it. God knows I don't want to carry Linda inside me like a ruptured organ for the rest of my life. I don't want to love her. But I very much need to *have loved* her. I don't want some new nothing to seem in my mind to have been nothing always. I don't want to look at her and see just a thin, bewildered woman, her roots growing out brownly, the caps on her teeth darkening, her hips widening, her fingers hooked like talons around a beer can, a cigarette, or the telephone receiver. I need to look at her and feel a warmth for someone once loved, my wife, my friend, mother of my kids, and all the rest of the civilized, in-between crap. But, buddy, I know even as I think it that it just ain't gonna be that way. It will be some kind of a living thing until it's finally killed. Then it will be a dead thing. *No* thing. *Nothing*. Jesus.

CHAPTER NINETEEN

Am I well? Getting well? Yes, I suppose. He recovered from his illness but the medicine killed him. I *am* well, of course. I am as well, my friend, as I ever was and as well, I suppose, as I'll ever be. This may not be, in an absolute sense, very well. It may be, in fact, a spectacular unwellness. But so what? Let's stop bidding for the three-story brick house. Let's settle for a brick at a time, or just one brick total. Or a pile of brick dust. Let's settle for anything, whatever is at hand, whatever's available. Let's stop blueprinting and architecting and building. Screw all that. Let's just *be*. And accept. Then stop being. And accept that.

Do you think I can pull it off, me the king of the architects and scaffold-builders and what-about-tomorrow speakers? Sure I can, buddy. You bet your ass I can.

I will ride that God-damned subway to Fordham Road until the wheels grind off or rust off, I'll take Gregg and Arthur to the park to swing and seesaw and climb the monkey bars until they're fifty, I'll keep those weekly checks humming through the mails, I'll go on all the dull-assed, fruitless interviews my agent suggests, I will do bad roles on television for little money just to please, I will even wear gray suits and striped ties and sit behind a desk composing selling messages if that must be done. I will work nights at home painting pictures for Linda to store or sell or swap to the shoe-store people for black kid pumps.

I will do all this in high spirits and good humor, carrying no musk of the martyr around with me. I will be cheerful and cooperative and self-sacrificing, striving to please all those I come in contact with. I will stand for the Salvation Army and Alcoholics Anonymous and testify loudly that my old gods were false gods. I will be and do what my fellow men in their wisdom decide that I should. I will lead a clean, sober life without peaks or hollows and I will try to die with freshly shampooed hair and empty bowels so as not to inconvenience the mortician. Don't laugh, you son of a bitch. I might do it. I might do it all.

Gregg spent last weekend with me. When he walked into the apartment ("This is an *old* building, Daddy"), he opened his bag, took out a picture of a donkey wearing a sombrero and said, "Here. I brought a picture for your wall."

We stuck it up on the fireplace with four strips of drafting tape. Saturday afternoon, I took him to see a play for children, *Rumpelstiltskin*, and on Sunday we visited friends uptown. He is very old for four.

Alicia came back from her holiday Monday. I met her at five in the lounge of an uptown hotel on Madison Avenue. She was very brown from the sun. And reserved. Quietly angry, in fact, because I hadn't written to her in New Orleans. We sat in the dark bar of the hotel and drank dry vermouth and when the conversation limped at last to a halt, I walked with her to her apartment building, took her upstairs, and made love to her on the living-room carpet. "You *did* miss me, didn't you?" she said. She mixed me a drink then and I read the paper while she went into the kitchen and started cooking dinner.

April is showing its tender middle now. It rains nearly

every day. I have a rotten cold but my eyes don't hurt as much as they did. Tomorrow I'm taking Gregg and Arthur to the circus at Madison Square Garden. It's my afternoon to report to the unemployment office so I'll have to figure out something to tell those folks when I come in a day late.

Saturday morning, Arthur will be here to spend the weekend with me. Gregg was here last, so this week it's Arthur's turn.

THE END